THE MIRACULOUS

The MIRACULOUS

Jess Redman

SQUARE
FISH

FARRAR STRAUS GIROUX · NEW YORK

SQUARE
FISH

An imprint of Macmillan Publishing Group, LLC
120 Broadway, New York, NY 10271
mackids.com

Our books may be purchased in bulk for promotional, educational, or business use.
Please contact your local bookseller or the Macmillan Corporate and Premium Sales Department
at (800) 221-7945 ext. 5442 or by email at MacmillanSpecialMarkets@macmillan.com.

Library of Congress Cataloging-in-Publication Data

Names: Redman, Jess, 1986– author.
Title: The miraculous / Jess Redman.
Description: New York : Farrar, Straus and Giroux, 2019. | Summary: After losing his faith
    in miracles after the death of his newborn sister, eleven-year-old Wunder Ellis meets a
    mysterious old woman who needs his help to reconnect the living and the dead,
    bringing himself and his town face-to-face with miracles.
Identifiers: LCCN 2018020006 | ISBN 978-1-250-25036-0 (paperback) |
    ISBN 978-0-374-30975-6 (ebook)
Subjects: | CYAC: Miracles—Fiction. | Grief—Fiction. | Death—Fiction. | Family life—
    Fiction. | Friendship—Fiction.
Classification: LCC PZ7.1.R4274 Mi 2019 | DDC [Fic]—dc23
LC record available at https://lccn.loc.gov/2018020006

Originally published in the United States by Farrar Straus Giroux
First Square Fish edition, 2020
Book designed by Elizabeth H. Clark
Square Fish logo designed by Filomena Tuosto

LEXILE: 650L

For my father,
who believed in this story
and in me
from the very beginning,
and who taught me
to approach this miraculous world
with curiosity, humility, and a sense of wonder.

here is the deepest secret nobody knows
(here is the root of the root and the bud of the bud
and the sky of the sky of a tree called life; which grows
higher than soul can hope or mind can hide)
—E. E. Cummings

Truly, we live with mysteries too
marvelous to be understood.
—Mary Oliver

Part One
THE BIRD

Chapter 1

On the night before the funeral, Wunder Ellis stopped believing in miracles.

Before that, he had really and truly believed. In fact, he had been a miracologist.

He became a miracologist when he was five years old. It happened like this:

It was dusk, and he was walking with his mother and father through the woods on the edge of Branch Hill. He had been in the woods before—the woods full of sprawling oaks and knobbly kneed cypresses and Spanish moss that cascaded down branch after branch like so many gray-green waterfalls.

He had been in the woods before. But he had always stayed close to his parents.

That evening, full of after-dinner ice cream and end-of-the-day adventurousness, he ran ahead.

He ran down the path that was potholed and cracked, but paved nonetheless. Above him, a bird cawed out a sunset song.

Then he came to a particularly toweringly tall live oak. It was covered in brilliant green resurrection fern, and beside it there was a dirt trail.

From the path he could see that the trail led to a house, a house in the middle of the woods. He could still hear his parents not far behind him—his father's voice low and slow, his mother's faster and full of dips and rises. They were so close that he felt brave.

Brave enough to turn down the trail.

The house was like nothing Wunder had ever seen—a ramshackle, crumble-tumble collection of widow's walks and towers and sagging porches and broken windows. It was made of a wood that looked black in the fading light.

Except for the grain of the wood, which was circular and so pale that it nearly glowed, covering the house in bright white spirals.

There was a sign hanging in the overgrown clearing in

front of the house. Wunder couldn't read yet, but he knew his letters, and he had found *D*, *W*, and *H* when he heard the bird from above cawing again.

The bird from above now cawing below.

Cawing very close to him.

Before he could duck, he felt something brush past the top of his head, soft, soft, feather soft, and then the bird was above him. A white shape soaring up to the peak of the very tallest tower.

And as the bird landed, the wood-grain spirals—from the top of the house to the bottom—began to turn. Slowly at first, then faster and faster until they were spinning so wildly that Wunder felt dizzy.

Spinning like thousands of clock hands. Spinning like thousands of tops set off at once.

Wunder had heard about miracles his entire life. He had been one, after all—the baby who should not have been born. But he had never seen one himself until right then.

And as he watched with wide blue eyes, he felt something lift off inside him. It was as if that bird hadn't flown past him but instead had burst out of his own heart and was now fluttering through him, making his fingertips and the end of his nose tingle, muffling sound with its feathers. He was suddenly aware of how marvelous, how mysterious everything around him was, suddenly aware of how he was a part of that. He was filled, he knew, with a miracle feeling.

Then the bird cawed again.

The spinning stopped.

And up in that tallest tower, Wunder saw something move. A shadow in the window.

He turned and ran back down the trail.

"The house!" he cried. "Spinning! Someone's in there!"

His parents were only a few feet ahead of where the dirt trail met the paved path. They listened as he told them what had happened.

"That's the DoorWay House," his father said. "But no one lives there."

"It does look pretty magical though, doesn't it?" his mother said, peering down the trail herself.

Wunder tried to explain again. His parents smiled and nodded some more. He could tell they didn't really believe him.

But he knew what he had seen. He knew what he had felt. And more than anything, he realized, he wanted to have that feeling again.

The heart-bird feeling.

He wanted to find another miracle.

"I want to be a miracler," he told his parents. "I mean, a miraclist. No, a mira . . . mirac . . ."

"Miracologist?" his father suggested.

"Miracologist," Wunder said slowly, testing out the word. "Miracologist." He nodded. "That's it. I want to be a miracologist."

His mother laughed and put her arm around him. "Well, of course you do."

"I bet Father Robles knows all about miracles," his father said. "We can talk to him on Sunday."

"And I'll help you learn about the not-church ones," his mother said as they started back down the path in the fast-falling darkness. "There are miracles happening all the time, all around us. And if anyone can find them, it's you, my Wunder."

They bought him a journal the very next day—black leather with silver-edged pages and the title he had chosen stamped on the cover in white:

THE MIRACULOUS

As the years passed, Wunder filled *The Miraculous* with stories—his own and those he collected—with interviews of neighbors, with newspaper articles, with verses from holy books, with quotes from philosophers that he didn't fully understand.

And with every page, Wunder was full of the feeling that

the world was wonderful, the feeling that he was not alone, the feeling that he was not just himself—not just Wunder Ellis—but something else too.

Something lighter, something brighter, something lifted.

He was filled with the heart-bird feeling.

So yes, Wunder Ellis had believed in miracles. He had really and truly believed.

Until the night before the funeral.

Chapter 2

On that night, the night before the funeral, Wunder still
believed in miracles as he tried for the hundredth time to
start the schoolwork he had missed over the last two weeks.
His earth sciences book was open in front of him. It had
been open for two hours, and in those hours, he had read
the title of the chapter—"Trees of the World"—and he had
stared at the pictures.

Live oak. Sacred fig. Yew. Ash.

Wunder stared at the pictures until branches and leaves
and trunks blurred together, until greens and browns faded
into a dark gray spot.

Then he closed the book.

He still believed in miracles as he said good night to his father, who was sitting on the living room couch, a blanket and pillow beside him. His father had spent the evening staring at papers of his own—not "Trees of the World" but hospital bills and bank statements and a list of expenses for the funeral that Wunder's mother did not want to have. When Wunder said good night, his father reached out his hand, but he didn't look up from the paper-strewn coffee table.

Wunder placed his hand in his father's for a moment.

Then he let go and left the living room.

He still believed in miracles as he walked down the hallway, past his parents' bedroom. The lights were off, the room was silent, and Wunder knew the door was still locked. His mother was inside. She had spent most of her time in her room since there was no longer any reason to spend most of her time in a hospital room.

Wunder paused. He pressed his hand to the door frame.

Then he went to his door, and he opened it.

And it was then, at that exact moment, that he stopped believing in miracles.

For the last five nights, Wunder had slept out on the couch. He had gone into his room only when necessary—to grab a new shirt, to put away his pillow.

But he couldn't sleep on the couch tonight, because his father was sleeping out there. His father was sleeping out there because when he told Wunder's mother that he had arranged the funeral she did not want, she had locked the door to their bedroom.

Wunder had been sleeping out there because of what was in the far corner of his room.

And looking at it now, his heart absolutely did not feel like a bird. His heart felt like a broken promise. His heart felt like a stone, hard and cold and heavy.

Then he looked around the rest of his room. It was, he realized, a miracologist's room. But now, he wasn't a miracologist anymore.

He knew what he had to do.

He went to the walls first. Down came the framed picture of himself as a baby, the words *Where there is great love there are always miracles* inscribed along the bottom. Down came a drawing of the Twin Miracle of the Buddha that he'd traced from a library book. Down came the Calendar of the Saints, still showing September 26, as if time had stopped on that day.

Then he cleared off his desk, which was covered in the newspapers he scoured daily for stories of miracles. He tossed an old clipping from the *Branch Hill Broadcast* about his miracology. There was a copy of the speech he'd written for the first meeting of the Unexplainable and Inexplicable Phenomenon Society there too. He'd started the club at the beginning of the school year, and so far that first meeting was the only one he'd had.

Now he was sure he would never have another one.

From the bookshelf, he took down the eleven angel statues his father had given him, one for each year of his life. Then he started on the books—poetry, philosophy, scriptures from many faiths—all filled with miracles, all given to him over the years by teachers and family and neighbors.

He tossed them to the floor, one by one.

Then there was only one thing left. On his nightstand, worn black leather with a peeling white title—*The Miraculous*.

He picked up the book. He ran his fingers along the silver edges, along the letters stamped on its front, then opened it to the first page. The writing there was his mother's, because he hadn't known how to write yet:

Miraculous Entry #1

My name is Wunder Ellis, and I am a miracologist. My mother says my birth was a miracle, but I don't remember that. The first miracle that I remember

happened yesterday. I was in the woods, and there was
a bird—

Wunder slammed the book shut. He didn't want to read about miracles. He didn't want to read his first entry, and he definitely didn't want to read his last entry—the entry he'd completed five days ago, before he knew there would be a funeral.

He didn't want to read *The Miraculous*. So he threw it into the pile of discarded things.

He threw it as hard as he could.

Then he rolled everything up inside the rug and shoved it into his closet, behind his shoes, behind his laundry hamper, in the very back where he wouldn't have to see it.

Now his room felt like the stone of his heart. Cold. Bare. Dark.

Except for the far side of the room.

The far side of the room, where the bright, soft promise of something new stood.

The crib.

The crib was still there.

"She'll be in our room at first," his mother had said just two months ago. Her face had been pink and glowing. "But once she outgrows her bassinet—once she's sleeping through the night—what do you think about her being in your room?"

Wunder had been expecting this question, and he was ready with his answer.

"Yes," he had told his mother. "Yes, I'd like that."

And the heart-bird had soared through him.

But she never slept there, in the white crib with the flower-patterned sheet that his mother had washed over and over to take the scratchiness out of it.

She never slept in the bassinet either, the bassinet next to his parents' bed, ready and waiting for someone small.

She never made it home.

And if that wasn't proof that miracles didn't exist, Wunder didn't know what was.

Chapter 3

The next morning, Wunder and his father walked silently
through the woods together. Wunder had his hands in the
pockets of his black pants. He was cold in the early-
autumn air, especially in the shade of the trees, because
he hadn't worn his jacket. His jacket was sky blue, and
sky blue was not a funeral color.

His father was wearing khaki pants and an olive wind-
breaker, but he couldn't help it. Wunder's mother still had
not unlocked the door.

Wunder had now been in the woods hundreds of times.
He rode his bicycle through them to and from school every
day. They weren't really on the way—in fact, they were

very much out of the way. But he liked to stop at the toweringly tall live oak and stare down the dirt path, stare through the leaves and limbs at the DoorWay House.

Just looking at the house had always been enough to give Wunder the heart-bird feeling. And he had always hoped that one day, he would see the spinning again. Or even hear the cawing bird.

What he had never thought much about was what was on the other side of the woods—Branch Hill Cemetery.

Now that was all he could think about. He didn't even glance at the DoorWay House as they walked past. He knew there would be no spinning today.

The woods ended at the cemetery gates. Inside them, a man in a long white robe was waiting. The man was very, very old with a stooped back and a frizzy halo of dark gray hair and glasses with thick black rims. In one hand he clutched a wooden cane. In the other he held some papers. With a scowl, he thrust them toward Wunder's father.

"Are you Mr. Ellis?" he cried. "You're late, you know! And where is the mother? Where are the other mourners? Here, take these."

Wunder's father took the papers, then stood, staring in confusion at the old man.

"Where's Father Robles?" he asked.

"What?" the old man yelled.

"Father Robles!" Wunder's father said, louder. "He's supposed to be here."

"Father Robles is out of town, you know! Come along!" The old man began to hobble down the cemetery path.

Wunder looked up at his father, who was frowning now.

"Well, then, where's Deacon Brannon?"

"They're together! Meeting with the bishop, you know. Very important. That's why I'm here."

"But who are you?"

The old man didn't answer.

"Who are you?" Wunder's father yelled.

"I'm the Minister of Consolation, of course!" the old man cried over his shoulder. "I'm here to minister, you know. I'm here to console. So let's get started!"

The minister turned off the path and into the grass at the base of the cemetery's hill. Wunder's father seemed like he was about to protest further. But then he sighed a deep sigh and followed the minister, his hand on Wunder's shoulder.

"Maybe it's a good thing your mother didn't come," he said.

Wunder had to agree. This very unconsoling Minister of

17

Consolation would not have changed his mother's mind. He certainly wasn't changing Wunder's.

Wunder hadn't understood before why his mother was so opposed to the funeral, why she had sent her parents and her sister home, why she had refused to speak to visitors, why she had shut herself in her room. But after last night, he understood. Because now he felt the same way.

He didn't want to listen to anyone read verses or pray or talk about how his sister was in a better place. He didn't want to see the casket or the grave. He was glad no one else had been invited. He didn't want to be there at all.

So when the minister tapped his fuzzy temple and yelled, "I have the whole rite up here! The beginning is 'Dear friends, death shows us how little we truly know' or something like that," Wunder shoved his hands into his pockets and tried to stop listening. He didn't look at the minister. He didn't look down. He stared, instead, at the top of the hill.

The cemetery's hill was *the* Branch Hill, the hill the town was named for. There were, however, no branches on top of Branch Hill. No trees. Not even a bush. While the minister yelled his way through the greeting, Wunder imagined each of the trees of the world up there, one after another.

When he ran out of trees, he let his gaze drift back down

the hill. There was another family there, a short, dark-haired woman and two girls standing in a semicircle around a gray gravestone. They were the only other people in the cemetery. All three wore black, but the smallest girl's dark clothing billowed around her, like a flag, a black flag. Wunder thought he recognized her.

"'Behold! I tell you a miracle'!"

Wunder turned from the empty hill and the girl with the black-flag clothing.

"'We will not all sleep, but we will all be changed'!"

The minister bellowed these words. The sun was behind him, lighting up his halo of gray hair and his white robe.

Wunder felt the stone of his heart—cold, dark, and heavy—grow suddenly, slightly warmer.

Then the sun disappeared behind a cloud. The world became dark again.

Wunder glanced over at his father and found that he was crying. Silent crying, tears drip, drip, dripping. Wunder watched as one teardrop slipped off the end of his nose, past the papers he clutched, which read RITE OF FINAL COM- MENDATION FOR AN INFANT. Down fell the teardrop, down toward the ground, down where Wunder had been trying not to look.

There was the grave.

And there was the casket—bright white, shiny, so small. He hadn't known they made caskets that small. He wasn't sure what he'd expected exactly—a normal-size one maybe, like there were at funerals in movies.

But, of course, that wouldn't make sense. She wouldn't need all that space.

As long as there were caskets so small, there were no miracles.

The stone of his heart went cold, cold, colder than cold again.

"Consolation, you know, and comfort and peace and good things!" the Minister of Consolation cried.

"Amen," Wunder's father said.

Wunder was silent.

"I have found that it can be consoling," the minister said, "for the bereaved to put some dirt on the casket. Ashes to ashes, dust to dust, as they say. So you can do that now, if you want."

Wunder did not want to do that. He did not feel like it would be consoling, not at all. But his father's hand was still on his shoulder, and there were still tears drip, drip, drip-ping from his eyes. So Wunder went with him.

There was a pile of earth on the other side of the grave.

Wunder and his father each took a handful and placed it on top of the casket.

Like they were planting something.

Like something alive was going to rise out of the ground.

But it wasn't.

She wasn't.

His sister was dead.

Chapter 4

The sun was behind them as they left the grave site.
Wunder could feel it on his back. Ahead of him, there were
long dark shadows.

He fell behind as his father and the minister crossed the
grass to the path that ran through the cemetery.

"But where is the mother?" the minister was yelling, even
though Wunder's father had already explained that she had
chosen not to come. "She should be here, you know!"

The other family was leaving too. The taller girl and the
woman were ahead of his father and the minister. Their
arms were linked, and they walked briskly, leaning into the
wind.

The smaller girl was far behind them, still near the grave site her family had been gathered around. She was moving so slowly that at first Wunder didn't realize she was moving at all. With every step, she dragged her black-sneakered toes along the grass. But when she saw Wunder coming down the path, she sped up—just slightly.

Soon they were walking side by side.

"I know you," the girl said, and her voice was slow and dreamy, like someone sleep-talking. "You're Wunder. We go to school together."

Up close, Wunder definitely recognized her. She was very recognizable. She had black hair cut into a bob, and her overgrown bangs hung into her eyes, which were ringed in smudgy black, raccoon-like. She wore lacy black gloves with the fingers cut off.

And perhaps her most defining feature: She wore a long black cloak. Not just in cemeteries either. All the time. Wunder had heard Vice Principal Jefferson hollering through the halls about that cloak. It was against the dress code.

"We do," Wunder said. "Faye."

"That's right," Faye said. "Faye Ji-Min Lee. I came to the first meeting of your Unexplainable and Inexplicable Phenomenon Society."

"I remember," Wunder said.

What he remembered was that at the first meeting of the UIPS, Faye had been the only attendee, other than Wunder's two best friends, Davy and Tomás. She had arrived late and had promptly climbed on top of one of the desks. After settling her cloak around her, she had sat, cross-legged, silent, and expressionless, for the entire meeting. At the end, she had climbed down, leaned closer to Wunder than he felt comfortable with, and said, "I don't know how I feel about your excessive smiling. And I was hoping to hear more about the darker side of supernatural activity. But I'm glad you started this club. I'll attend the next meeting."

Wunder hadn't been sure how he felt about her then, but he knew one thing for sure—he did not want to talk to her now.

He sped up.

But so did Faye.

"We're here because it's my grandfather's birthday," she said. "Well, it would have been. He's been dead for a hundred and seven days."

"Oh," Wunder said. "I'm sorry."

Faye waved one black-gloved hand slowly, languidly. "You didn't kill him, did you, Wundie?"

Then she stared at him until he felt like he had to say something. "No," he said. "No, I didn't. And it's Wunder, not Wundie. No one calls me that."

Faye didn't seem to have heard him. "Is this the funeral? Ms. Shunem told everyone about your sister in science class. Did you know we're in the same science class? Why isn't anyone else here? Is that a priest?" She waved her black-gloved hand ahead of her now. "There's no priest at our church, just a pastor. Well, it's really my mother's church. I go sometimes, and my grandfather did too, but he was very open to other ideas, and so am I. I happen to be interested in the paranormal—ghosts, vampires, banshees, et cetera."

This string of questions and information was delivered in a dreamy monotone, and at the end of it, Wunder found himself openmouthed but at a loss for words.

So he decided not to say anything. He closed his mouth and shrugged.

Faye shrugged back at him. "Well, your priest is extremely strange," she said.

"He's not a priest," Wunder said. "He's a Minister of Consolation."

"Consolation? Really?" Faye's raccoon eyes considered the minister, who was shuffling along beside Wunder's father and yelling, "What about the other mourners, you know? Quite unusual. Why even have a funeral?"

"I wonder," she said, "if the person who hired him knows what that word means."

Wunder almost smiled at this, but then he didn't. He didn't want to smile in the cemetery, on the day of his sister's funeral, and he didn't want to encourage Faye to keep talking.

"We could hear him from my grandfather's grave," she said. "He's very loud. But I did like that one verse, 'Behold! I tell you a miracle'!"

This last part, Faye screamed.

Wunder's father and the minister jerked to a stop. They turned and stared at Faye. Wunder stared at her too.

Faye stared back, seemingly unfazed.

She waited until Wunder's father and the minister finally started walking again, then continued, "It was very dramatic, like an incantation or a spell. Almost supernatural. I'm extremely sensitive to the supernatural. I'm sure you are too."

Wunder didn't reply.

"With a name like yours, Wundie," Faye said, "you have no choice but to believe in signs and wonders."

"Well, I don't," Wunder said. "I mean, I used to. But I don't anymore. And it's Wunder, not Wundie."

Faye stopped her sneaker-dragging walk and stood stock-still. Wunder stopped too, before he really thought about it, and watched as Faye pulled a bobby pin from her cloak and pinned her bangs back. She studied him, eyes now unobstructed.

"You're different now, aren't you?" she said. "At the meeting you were so"—her face morphed into a crazy, huge grin and she pumped one fist in the air—"zippy." The grin disappeared. Her fist sank slowly back to her side. "You're not very zippy anymore."

Wunder didn't answer. He turned back to the shadowy path. He knew it was true. He used to be able to talk to anyone, especially about the miraculous. But now it was as if parts of him had been erased, blacked out, like he was a checkerboard inside. He couldn't seem to find words. He didn't even want to find them.

"Come along, young man!" The Minister of Consolation was shouting at him now. His white robe looked gray.

Wunder hurried forward, relieved to leave Faye behind.

He stayed close to his father as they headed into the woods. He could hear Faye behind him, her cloak snapping in the wind, her feet scuff, scuff, scuffing along, but he didn't turn around. When they passed the dirt trail, he kept his head lowered so he wouldn't look down it, down to the DoorWay House. He didn't want to see it.

Then, very close to him, there came a sound: *Caw!*

Wunder ducked and threw his arms up. Behind him,

Faye let out a high, sharp laugh. Something brushed past his head, something soft, light, feathery.

When he straightened up, he saw the bird flying down the trail that led to the DoorWay House. Its black shape disappeared behind the house's tallest tower.

And for a moment—a split second—he thought he saw the spirals shifting.

Then they were still.

But someone was there.

Not in the tower though. On the porch.

In a rocking chair made of the same black spiraling wood as the house, there was an old woman. She was dressed in white, in a sort of robe with shawls and belts, and she had long black hair that was blowing wildly around her. A newspaper was spread out on her lap. Its pages flapped like wings.

As Wunder gaped at her, the old woman looked up from her paper. Her head turned slowly until her eyes found him.

She smiled. Then she lifted one hand. And she waved.

Wunder jerked his gaze away. He turned to his father and the minister. But neither of them was looking at the Door-Way House.

Farther ahead, Mrs. Lee and her older daughter walked

on, their heads bent together. They weren't looking at the DoorWay House either.

But, behind him, Faye had stopped in the middle of the path. She had pulled the hood of her cloak up, and she was staring out from under its peak. Staring past the live oak, down the dirt trail, through the leaves and branches and vines at the DoorWay House.

The old woman was still there. Her hand was still raised. Her hair had whipped across her face, covering her eyes.

But Wunder knew she was still watching him.

Chapter 5

That night Wunder's father heated up one of the many casseroles that had been pouring into the house since Wunder's sister was born, this one from someone named Mariah Lazar. Wunder set two places at the kitchen table, one for him and one for his father. His mother was still in her room.

Wunder didn't like peas. He didn't like cauliflower either. Those and some chunks of unidentifiable meat seemed to be the only ingredients in the casserole.

But he didn't feel like eating anyway. There were too many feelings filling him up, too many thoughts distracting him.

"Did you hear what the Minister of Consolation said?" he asked his father after pushing green blobs of food around his plate for a few minutes.

Wunder's father sniffed his forkful of casserole. "I did. I think everyone in Branch Hill did."

"But did you hear the part—the part about the miracle? I've never heard that verse."

Wunder's father took a tentative bite, then set his fork right back down. "That minister said a lot of words— screamed a lot of words, actually—but I don't know if he meant any of them." He picked up his fork again. "Father Robles must have forgotten that the funeral was today. I know he wanted to be there. I would have liked for him to have been there. And our friends and family too."

Wunder didn't want to tell his father that he didn't feel the same way, that he understood now why his mother hadn't wanted to have the funeral. So he let silence fill the room again before saying, "Remember when I thought I saw someone in the DoorWay House when I was little? It was strange to see someone there today, wasn't it?"

Wunder's father set his empty fork down again. "Some- one was there?"

"The old woman," Wunder said. "On the porch."

"I didn't see her," Wunder's father said. "That house should have been torn down years ago."

He stood up, collected his paper plate and Wunder's, then dumped both in the trash. "What do you say we try a different casserole?"

After dinner, Wunder's father went to the living room and spread out his papers. Wunder sat with him, trying and failing to do his homework again, until the telephone rang.

Wunder's father came from a big family that was spread out all over the country, and they had been calling every day since Wunder's sister was born. His mother's parents and her sister, Aunt Anita, lived across the state, and they had been calling every day since Wunder's mother had asked them to leave. All of them, Wunder was sure, would want to know about the funeral.

He didn't want to be the one to tell them about it.

He headed to his room, but thoughts of the funeral followed him anyway. He kept picturing the old woman on the porch and remembering the shadow in the window. He kept feeling the feathers of the bird and hearing the minister's thundering words.

Behold! I tell you a miracle.

Last night, he had been so angry, angry enough to

stop believing in miracles, angry enough to put away *The Miraculous*.

But so much had happened today that he wasn't only angry anymore. More than anything, he was confused.

Then he opened his door, and there was the crib.

He felt only angry again.

This time, at himself. Because it was the day of his sister's funeral and he was already thinking about miracles again.

He went to his closet and unrolled the rug enough to yank out the black-and-white leather-covered book. Then he shoved it into his backpack, which sat by his newly cleared-off desk.

Tomorrow, he was going to get rid of *The Miraculous*. For good.

That night, Wunder fell asleep staring at the shadows of the crib bars on the floor.

And he had a dream.

In his dream, the crib-bar shadows stretched out, longer and longer. They split and came together, crossing, weaving, interlacing—tree branches.

A darker shadow appeared, perched in the branch shadows. The shape of a bird.

Caw! the shadow bird cawed. *Caw! Caw!*

Wunder woke up. He didn't recognize his room. The walls were blank. His angel statues weren't watching over him.

And the crib-bar shadows had reached his bed. They stretched out over his whole blanket-covered body.

He closed his eyes and tried not to think.

But he didn't fall back to sleep for a long, long time.

Part Two

THE STONE

Chapter 6

Wunder had been out of school since the day of his sister's birth.

If she had been born healthy, he probably would have been back in class the next day. But on the day she was born, the doctors had told his parents that she wasn't going to live for long. His mother hadn't believed them, but she had wanted Wunder to be there anyway, in the hospital room, getting to know his sister.

But now his sister was gone and the funeral was over, and it was time for Wunder to go back to school.

He didn't want to go back. He didn't want to listen to everyone say how sorry they were. He didn't want to pretend that he was fine, just fine.

But he didn't want to stay home.

His father left for work very early. The sound of the front door closing woke Wunder out of an unsettled half sleep.

His mother did not have to be back to work for four more weeks. She had been on maternity leave.

Now she was on bereavement leave.

Wunder knew that she wouldn't leave her room, but it didn't matter. She didn't have to be in the same room for him to feel her sadness. It seeped under closed doors, spread across floors, filled up every vacant space. Her sadness was a thing Wunder felt he could drown in.

It seemed impossible that a few weeks ago, she had been so happy, happier than he had ever seen her. A few weeks ago, she had looked, all the time, the way she did when she told the story of Wunder's birth.

Wunder had heard that story more times than he could count. It was in *The Miraculous*, of course. It was in there several times, with more details as he grew older. His mother had written a version over the summer, while she was pregnant. It went like this:

Miraculous Entry #1279

You know, Wunder,· this is my favorite story. The story of you.

It starts with me and your father. We were high school sweethearts, and we got married right after graduation. This, as you know, is not something I recommend, Wunder, although it's not something that I regret.

After a few years, we wanted to have a baby, even though we were babies ourselves. Again, not something I recommend, but we felt—your dad and I—that we had so much love, too much love for just the two of us.

But year after year after year, there was no baby. We tried everything we could afford. We went to so many doctors. Your father prayed and lit a million candles at St. Gerard's. I drank special teas and went on fertility retreats and tried my best not to worry so much. But nothing worked.

Until, after ten years—unexplainably, inexplicably— we found out that you were on the way.

I won't lie to you, Wunder; it was a hard pregnancy. I was sick the whole time, and there were a lot of concerns about your health.

But then you were born—a fuzzy-headed, blue-eyed, seven-pound pooping machine, as Dad always says— and you were perfect. You were absolutely perfect, and we were so in love with you.

And you know your father has always had so much faith, always believed so easily and so strongly. And you know that before you were born, I never really believed in much of anything.

But when I met you, I couldn't deny that you were a miracle.

You were our Wunder.

Wunder had been enraptured by this story when he was young—the story of how wanted he had been, how longed for, the story of his specialness, of how he had defied the odds and come into being. As he got older, he started trying to cut his mother off when she told it, embarrassed by how she would run her hands over his hair and his back, how she would beam at him. But she never let him stop her, and he didn't really try that hard.

Embarrassed or not, he had always believed her. He was a miracle. Miracles happened.

And when his mother had announced, out of the blue, that she was pregnant, it had seemed like another miracle.

Not right away, of course. He'd had almost eleven years of only-child-hood, almost eleven years at the center of his parents' love, and at first, the news that everything was about to change had completely terrified him.

But little by little, his parents' excitement had become his own. His father had told him story after story about growing up with two sisters and three brothers. His mother had taken him to one of her ultrasounds, where he had seen, for the first time, the baby that would be theirs.

And his parents, they hadn't seemed to love him any less. In fact, everyone seemed to have more love.

He had started wondering what kind of big brother he would be, and once they knew she was a girl, what kind of little sister she would be. He had found himself paying attention to babies he saw at the grocery store or at the park, found himself thinking about things he could teach her and how it would feel to have someone to take care of, someone new to love.

He had helped his father set up the crib and install the car seat. He had helped his mother shop for baby clothes and bibs.

And he, he alone, had chosen her name.

They had all been so happy, waiting for her to be born.

And even when there were more and more doctor's visits and more and more bad reports and more and more times when Wunder walked in on his mother with her head in her hands—even when the baby was born and so much was wrong and everyone was waiting, waiting for her to die—even then, Wunder had expected that there would be another miracle.

But there hadn't been.

And he couldn't stay in the house with his mother and the crib and those rising floodwaters of sadness.

So he grabbed his backpack, full of schoolbooks and *The Miraculous*, and he headed out the front door.

Chapter 7

Wunder usually rode his bike to Golden Fig Middle School, but that day he felt like walking. He decided not to take the route through the woods either. He didn't want to see the cemetery. He didn't want to see the DoorWay House. He headed straight to school.

It felt strange to be going back after being gone for two weeks. Much stranger than returning after a vacation. It wasn't just that time had passed. He was different now. He thought about how Faye had described him—*not zippy.* He didn't like the word *zippy* any more than he liked *excessive smiling*, but he knew what she meant. He had always been happy.

Now his insides were a checkerboard and his room was bare and he was planning on getting rid of his life's work. He was definitely different.

At school, his best friends, Tomás and Davy, were waiting by his locker.

"Hey, Wunder," Tomás said, flipping his hair back. Tomás had been doing more things like that since they started sixth grade, things like styling his hair very carefully and matching his shirts to his sneakers. "What's going on?"

Wunder couldn't think of an answer to this question. He hadn't talked to Tomás during the past two weeks—he hadn't talked to any friends—but Tomás's mother had come to the house the day before the funeral. She had brought flowers and a card and a huge casserole, and she had talked quietly to Wunder's father, had even knocked on Wunder's mother's door.

And Faye had said Ms. Shunem had told their class about the funeral. So Tomás knew. Everyone probably knew.

"Some things, I guess," Wunder finally said. "I mean, nothing. I don't know."

His voice sounded like it didn't belong to him. It sounded flat, like it had been squashed under something heavy and cold.

Standing a little behind Tomás, Davy didn't speak but gave a half wave and a half smile. Davy had not changed since they started sixth grade. His hair was as curly and unstyled as ever, he was still quiet and cautious, and he still carried his schoolbooks in the mailbag he used on his morning paper route, *Branch Hill Broadcast* written in bright red on the side.

"Do you want to go to the Snack Shack after school?" Tomás asked. "They got a new arcade game last week. It's like that super-old one, *Space Invaders*, but with a huge screen and lasers and stuff."

Wunder turned back to Tomás. "What?" he asked.

"The Snack Shack," Tomás repeated slower. Louder. "My mom said she'll drive us." He glanced over at Davy. "You've got to come. Otherwise it'll just be me and Davy again."

Davy gave an apologetic smile.

"Maybe," Wunder said. He put his hands in his pockets. "I might be able to do that. I might not, but maybe."

Tomás seemed satisfied with this. He flipped his hair and headed toward English class. Wunder and Davy followed. Davy still didn't say anything, but he kept sneaking looks at Wunder, front teeth gnawing on his bottom lip, both hands gripping the strap of his bag.

Wunder had been worried that they would ask him about

45

his sister. But he hadn't thought about what he would do if they didn't.

He wasn't as surprised about Tomás. Tomás almost never asked about Wunder's weekend or his family or anything that didn't have to do with Tomás. Wunder wouldn't have said this aloud, but he sometimes thought that if he and Tomás hadn't met when they were little, they would never be friends now.

But Davy—Davy's mom had gotten cancer when they were in third grade. She didn't die, but she had been really, really sick. And Wunder had talked to him about it. Not a lot, but he hadn't pretended like it wasn't happening. He hadn't pretended like Mrs. Baum didn't exist.

All day, Wunder waited for one of them to say something, but they didn't say anything.

In fact, no one did.

Kids did look at him a lot more than usual—sneaky glances out of the corners of their eyes. A few gave him sympathetic looks, their mouths turning up slightly, sadly. And in science class, Ms. Shunem said, "Oh, Wunder, welcome back! I almost didn't recognize you without your smile!"

But that was it.

Until the end of the day.

"Wundie, we need to talk."

Faye Ji-Min Lee was at his locker. She wore her black cloak and her lacy fingerless gloves, but instead of the black dress she had worn at the funeral, she had on jeans and a bright-yellow-and-pink-flowered blouse. It was, Wunder thought, a very incongruous ensemble.

"It's Wunder," he said. "Never Wundie. No one calls me Wundie."

"Wundie. Listen. Could you be quiet for two seconds, please?" Faye said. "It's rude to interrupt. And this is very important."

"Okay, but it's Wunder," Wunder said. "What's so important?"

As if in slow motion, Faye reached into her cloak, pulled out a bobby pin, and pinned back her bangs. Her eyes scanned the hallways—left, right, then left again. "About yesterday." She leaned toward him.

This was it. Someone was going to talk to him about the funeral, about his sister. Wunder felt himself simultaneously reaching forward and shrinking back.

"About the witch," Faye whispered.

This was not at all what Wunder had expected her to say.

"The witch?"

"At the DoorWay House," Faye said. "You saw her. I know you did."

Even when he had believed in miracles, Wunder had

47

never spent much time on Faye's reported paranormal interests: *ghosts, vampires, banshees, et cetera*. So he hadn't thought of the porch-sitting woman as a witch. But now that Faye said it, he realized that was exactly what she looked like.

But all he said was, "I saw an old woman. There's no such thing as witches."

"Oh, she's a witch," Faye said, waving her gloved hand in lazy dismissal. "She lives in the DoorWay House. She wears hangy scraps of white cloth. She smiles and waves at mourners. Et cetera. If that isn't witch behavior, I'll eat my cloak." She held up one side, then dropped it for unenthusiastic emphasis. "So obviously we have to go to that house."

This was even more unexpected. "No, we don't. We don't have to do anything."

"She's. A. Witch." These last words were punctuated with even-longer-than-usual pauses and uncomfortable stares. "And you're the president of the Unexplainable and Inexplicable Phenomenon Society. You must want to meet her."

"No, I don't. I don't care about her."

"Wundie." Faye leaned closer to him, much closer than he wanted her to be. He could see little lines of skin through the black smudges under her eyes. "I know you're going through a hard time right now. I know you're very sad. But listen—you don't think it's a coincidence that we saw this witch now, do you? The day of the funeral? On my grand-father's birthday? And your creepy priest screaming those verses? That deranged bird diving at your head? Et cetera? These are miracles, Wundie!"

Faye's voice had grown faster, faster and higher, as she recounted all the things that had made Wunder so confused last night, all the things he had been trying not to think about.

"They aren't miracles!" he said. "They aren't anything. There isn't—"

"Miss Lee!" Vice Principal Jefferson was barreling down the hallway. "Miss Lee, you are in violation of the dress code. Take off that cape!"

"We'll talk later, Wundie." Faye spun away from him, moving faster than he had ever seen her move. "It's a cloak!" she shrieked.

Then she ran down the hallway, her black cloak stream-ing behind her.

Chapter 8

As Wunder finished putting away his books, he tried not to hear Faye's words playing over and over in his mind. The verse. The bird. The witch.

He wished he had never talked to her. He slammed his locker shut and picked up his backpack. *The Miraculous* was still inside, still weighing him down.

Outside, Tomás and Davy were waiting in their usual spot by the stairs.

"Hey, Wunder," Tomás said. "Ready to go?" Davy hovered by his elbow, smiling hopefully. "Come on. I want to try to get the high score."

Wunder didn't know what to say. He couldn't go play

video games right now. It was like Tomás didn't remember what had happened. Or didn't care. He started to back away from his friends.

"Wait, Wunder." Davy spoke for the first time. His voice was a nervous squeak. "We haven't—I haven't seen you in—in forever. And I wanted to talk to you about—"

"Sorry, Davy," Wunder said. "I need—I have some things I have to—sorry."

He practically ran down the school steps. As he hurried away, he saw Faye at the bike rack. He thought again about what she had said. He opened his mouth to yell her name.

Then he closed it again. He walked faster, hands in his pockets.

He needed to be alone. He needed to get rid of *The Miraculous*. Now.

The sky was clear and the afternoon sun was so bright that the world looked washed out and unfamiliar as Wunder stumbled down the sidewalk, away from school. The voices of kids at the bike rack and by the buses faded behind him. He wasn't headed toward home. He wasn't exactly sure where he was going.

In town, things were quiet, and there was hardly any

traffic. Everyone was still inside, finishing the afternoon's work.

Wunder passed the town hall, a brick building with a fountain and a few saplings out front. Then he hurried past Safe and Sound Insurance, where his mother worked, and the Snack Shack, where Tomás and Davy were probably already shooting aliens.

He passed the library and the pharmacy and stores he had never been in. There were trash cans here and there on street corners, and he thought about tossing *The Miraculous* into one, but he didn't. None of them seemed like the right place.

He went through the downtown, through the residential section—and then he was in the woods.

In the woods, Wunder finally slowed down. He knew no one would be there. No one ever was. The leaves hadn't begun to change yet, and the light that filtered through them patchworked a green-tinted pattern on the path. A soft breeze made the Spanish moss sway and the oak leaves wave.

The woods, he thought, might be a good place to leave the book. He searched for the perfect spot as he walked. But he still couldn't find one.

Coming from this direction, he reached the cemetery

gates before the DoorWay House. He held on to the iron bars and peered in. Gravestones dotted the fields like crooked teeth in a massive, yawning jaw, like dominoes set up and ready to fall. So many graves. Mostly, he thought, the graves of older people, people who had lived long lives, but maybe there were some like his sister's.

Graves of the unknown or the barely known, graves of the lost.

He pulled on the gate and found that it wasn't locked. He wasn't sure if there were rules about visiting cemeteries. It felt wrong to go in, but he went in anyway.

He stopped at the first grave he came to. There was a simple headstone there. The words glinted gold, a metallic wink, a signal, a beacon shining out from the black background.

Vita mutatur, non tollitur, read the words at the top of the stone. Beneath that was a name—*Dalia Ramos*—and dates.

Wunder didn't know what the words meant, but he could read the dates. Dalia was eighty-two when she died.

Eighty-two seemed like a good number of years to live.

He thought of his sister's gravestone. It hadn't been made yet, but he knew what it would look like. His father had shown him. The dates were carved in polished white marble, and if anyone bothered to calculate how long she had lived, they would come up with eight. Eight days.

Eighty-two years. Eight days.

The wind blew, and the shadow of a cloud fell across the golden words. Wunder could barely read them anymore.

He straightened up and walked farther into the cemetery, pausing here and there to look at grave markers, to read dates. Micah Shunem, who had been thirty years old when he died and a *beloved son and brother*. Avery Lazar, whose headstone didn't have any dates, just a statue of a white bird, wings spread in flight. A gray stone monument with the name *Kobayashi* across the top and black script and the outlines of little flowers beneath.

The treeless hill rose up ahead of him, grass green and empty. Wunder considered going to the base of the hill, to his sister's grave. He wouldn't say a prayer for her, but maybe he could sit next to her grave here the way he had sat next to her in the hospital.

But the longer he stayed in the cemetery, the less he wanted to be there.

When Wunder used to write in *The Miraculous*, he would sometimes feel like he was doing a miracle of his own. He would feel like there was something special about bringing all those stories from all those people together. Like he was connecting the dots of each soul he wrote about—connecting them to himself and to one another and to everything that gave him the heart-bird feeling.

The cemetery, he thought as he drew closer and closer to the hill, was the exact opposite of *The Miraculous*. Each grave was its own entry, its own story. But instead of making the world seem wonderful, instead of making Wunder feel connected and loved and happy, these stories made him feel separate and lonely and angry.

Then it occurred to him that this was where he should leave *The Miraculous*. In the most unmiraculous place of all.

He should leave it here, and then never come back.

He knelt and pulled the black leather volume from his backpack.

Caw! Caw! Caw!

Wunder jumped as the sound echoed off the headstones. *The Miraculous* fell from his hands.

"It's just a bird," he said out loud, but his voice shook and the feeling that he was somewhere he should not be returned.

He leaped to his feet, grabbed his backpack, and ran to the gates.

The bird cawed again. Closer this time.

Wunder kept running. He was in the woods now, and it

was dark, so dark after the brightness of the cemetery that it was hard to see.

And then he was passing the toweringly tall live oak, and the bird was cawing again, cawing as it swooped down the dirt trail. He knew he shouldn't look, he didn't want to look, but he did—

And there she was. Rocking in that spiral-wood rocking chair. Newspaper spread open over her knees. The pages fluttering in the wind. Like wings, like the wings of a bird.

The witch of the DoorWay House.

And just like last time, she was watching him.

Just like last time, she met his eye. She smiled.

And she waved.

Chapter 9

Wunder's father called the house that afternoon to say he would be working late.

"There's tons of food in the fridge," he said. "You can heat up whatever you want for dinner."

"Okay," Wunder said. "Sure."

His father was quiet for a few seconds. "I know I should be there," he said. "But I've been gone for two weeks. There's a lot to catch up on."

"It's fine," Wunder said. "I'll be fine."

Wunder's father was an engineer at SunShiners, where he designed solar panels. He used to be a technician there. When Wunder was younger, he would go to work with his father, and they would take apart equipment—massive metal machines—and his father would explain how the pieces worked. How they fit together.

Then, when Wunder was seven, his father graduated from college after years of night classes and applied for the engineer position. Wunder had written about it in *The Miraculous*. It went like this:

Miraculous Entry #322

Yesterday, I lit a candle at church for my dad because he really wanted the engineer job.

Then today, he came home and told us he got it! There were a lot of other people trying to get that job, but they chose him. He's really happy about it, and so is my mom, and so am I.

Everyone said Wunder was like his mother—always smiling, always asking questions, always wanting to know more. They even looked alike, both tall with freckled noses and blue eyes and dark brown hair that would never lie flat.

Wunder's father, on the other hand, was quiet and serious, and even though he didn't mind Wunder's and his mother's questions, he didn't ask many himself. He was satisfied, he always said, with the answers he had.

They were so different, Wunder and his father.

But every week, they went to church together, sitting and standing and kneeling side by side. And Wunder had been sure that he had helped his father to get the job he loved. That miracle, he had felt, connected them to each other.

Now, sitting alone at the kitchen table, eating casserole made by, the card said, Jairus Jefferson, Wunder knew that he hadn't had anything to do with it. And now that he had shoved his angels into the closet, now that he never wanted to go to church again, now he wondered what would connect him to his father.

He was almost finished with the casserole—which wasn't so bad, a sort of taco salad—when his mother wandered into the kitchen.

"Wunder." She said it like she was surprised to see him, like she hadn't expected him to be there. "Are you alone?"

Wunder struggled to find the words to say. He wasn't sure which ones would be right. "Dad had to work late," he finally said.

"He should be here with you," his mother replied. She looked older and more tired than he had ever seen her.

"He missed so much work," Wunder said. "And I'm okay. I'm fine. I'm doing fine."

"I know you are." She took out a can of soup, opened it, and poured it into a bowl. "But he should be here. And I should be too—I know that." She wasn't looking at him anymore. She was looking at the floor, gripping her soup bowl. "I know I should have let your grandparents stay— for you. And Dad's family—I know they want to come so badly. But I need—I just need a little more time."

Then she hurried out of the room, taking the bowlful of cold soup with her. Wunder kept waiting for her to come back to heat it up, to come back for a spoon, but she never did.

And he was left wondering what would connect him to his mother too.

When he went to bed hours later, his parents' door was shut again. He put his ear to the wood, but he couldn't hear anything. His father wasn't home yet. And the crib-bar shadows were already reaching toward his bed.

Chapter 10

The next day, Wunder stood at the bike rack after school.
Around him, kids were climbing on buses or pedaling off
on bikes, but he couldn't leave yet.

Not until he decided if he was going back to the cemetery or not.

He knew he shouldn't go back. He had told himself he
would never go back.

But last night, the cemetery had been all he could think
about. The cemetery and *The Miraculous*, discarded so hast-
ily, so unceremoniously.

The cemetery, *The Miraculous*, and other things. Other
things that he was trying his best not to think about.

He could go back, he finally decided, but only to put *The Miraculous* in a final resting place. He could go back once more, then never again.

He was about to head that way when Faye came meandering over.

"Wundie," she said. She wore pressed white pants and a magenta sweater. Her black cloak fluttered behind her. "We need to talk."

"It's Wunder," Wunder said. "Never Wundie."

"Wundie. Listen. I'm going to stop you right there," Faye said. Her cloak was slipping off her shoulder, and she paused to adjust it. It took a long time. "We have more important things to discuss. I think you know what I mean."

"I don't want to go to the DoorWay House," Wunder said firmly, hoping that would end the conversation.

Faye's smudgy eyes widened. "Why not, Wundie?"

"It's Wun—never mind," Wunder said with a sigh. "Because I don't. There isn't—there's no witch."

Wunder said this, but when he thought of the woman sitting on her porch, it was now the word *witch* that popped into his head. That was what he was calling her to himself, whether he wanted to admit it or not.

"How can you say that, Wundie?" Faye's dreamy voice was starting to wake up. "After everything we've witnessed?"

Her voice was growing louder, sharper. "The priest's incantation! The killer bird! Et cetera! How can you refuse to investigate these inexplicable and unexplainable phenomena?"

"He wasn't a priest," Wunder replied. "He was a Minister of Consolation. And the other stuff is—it's ordinary stuff. Just a bird. Just an old lady living in an old house. That's all."

Faye glared at him. "An old lady living in the *DoorWay House*. That's not ordinary, Wundie. I hardly ever see anyone there!"

Wunder was so surprised that he almost gasped. Other than the shadow in the window and now the witch, he had never seen anyone in the DoorWay House—or heard of anyone who had. He started to ask, *What do you mean* hardly ever?

Then he remembered. He didn't believe in miracles, even the ones that had happened when he was five. He didn't want to know anything about the DoorWay House.

"Not hardly ever," he said, shaking his head. "Never. No one has ever lived there."

"I've seen things," Faye insisted.

Wunder shook his head again, this time harder. "You probably imagined whatever you think you saw," he said, as much to himself as to her.

"Don't tell me what I have and have not seen, Wundie!" Faye shrieked.

"Shh!" Kids were staring at them. He wanted to leave, but he was pretty sure she would follow him. She wasn't going to give up. "Fine." He sighed. "What is it you think you've seen?"

Faye gripped the sides of her cloak and leaned toward him. "Shadows crossing the windows," she said, her voice soft again, like they were telling secrets. "And my grandfather—" She stopped suddenly and threw the hood of her cloak over her head. She was silent, dead silent, for almost a minute. Wunder wondered if he should say something, do something. Then she flipped the hood off. "My grandfather said he saw those spirals moving once, spinning around." She gave a nod of victory. "What about that?"

For the first time since the day of the funeral, Wunder felt the stone of his heart warm. Faye had seen shadows in the DoorWay House, like he had. Faye's grandfather had seen the spirals spin, like he had.

But he didn't want any of it to be true. It couldn't be true. "No one has ever lived in that house before!" he cried. Now he was the loud one, he was the one kids were staring at.

Faye held up one finger menacingly. Wunder was sure

she was going to scream again. Or maybe jab him in the eyeball.

Instead, she took a deep breath through her nose. Her expression melted back into blankness. Her finger dropped. "Fine," she said. "There's absolutely nothing supernatural going on at the DoorWay House that we need to investigate. So let's just go on a nice, ordinary, boring walk instead, okay?"

Wunder thought about telling her that she couldn't come. But then he didn't.

Chapter 11

As they started through town, Wunder was trying not to do three things.

He was trying not to hear Faye's words in his head: *He saw those spirals moving.*

He was trying not to notice the stone of his heart, still not-so-cold inside him.

He was trying not to wonder if the witch would be on her porch again, waving at him.

He was trying, but he was failing on all three counts.

But Faye, unsurprisingly, was not going to let him stay in his own thoughts. "Where are we walking, Wundie?" she asked after less than a block of silent strolling.

"Just around," Wunder said vaguely.

"Around? What for? Exploring? Meditating? Achieving enlightenment? I know a lot about enlightenment. My grandfather and I talked about it sometimes. My mother didn't like that, but my grandfather was very open. He said that if you want enlightenment, you have to accept that nothing in this life is permanent." She paused. "I don't think I'm very enlightened."

Wunder thought about his sister. What was more impermanent than an eight-day-old baby? But did he accept that?

"I'm not trying to achieve enlightenment," he said. "I've been—" He glanced at her out of the corner of his eye. "I went back to the cemetery yesterday. I was thinking about going again."

"Three days in a row among the dead?" Faye shook her head slowly, her bangs brushing past her eyebrows and back. "That's pretty morbid, Wundie."

"No, it's not," Wunder protested. "I'm not—I had something to leave there, and I didn't get to—"

"There's nothing wrong with being morbid," Faye said. "Why not spend time in a graveyard?" She spread her arms out, a side of her cloak clutched in either black-gloved hand. "Let's go."

In the woods, the tips of the leaves were just beginning to turn red and gold. It was quiet there, and Branch Hill Cemetery was empty too, as usual.

"So what should we do?" Faye asked as they passed through the iron gate. Her voice was hushed, and Wunder wondered if she was feeling the same way he was—like they really shouldn't be there. "Aren't you supposed to visit graves all the time and pray for the dead in your religion?"

"I guess," Wunder said, although so far Faye's family was the only one he had seen there. "But I'm not going to do that. I'm not going to pray."

"I'm not here to make you pray, Wundie," Faye said.

Now that they were there, Wunder felt like he wanted to leave. The feeling of loneliness, of separateness he'd felt yesterday came over him again. All around were hundreds of monuments marking hundreds of dead bodies, each one sealed off, each one alone. It was terrible, almost too terrible to stand.

"We're surrounded by dead people," Faye said, almost as if she could read his mind. She pulled the hood of her cloak up.

"We are," he said.

"What's even stranger to think about," she said, "what I

thought about when I saw you at the funeral, is that almost everyone buried here has a family living in this town. Branch Hill is filled with families of the dead."

Wunder nodded, remembering. He remembered what he'd thought yesterday—that each grave was its own sad, lonely story. If each of those stories belonged to a family in Branch Hill, then his town must have hundreds of people like him and Faye, hundreds who didn't get their miracles.

Which was further proof, Wunder thought, that miracles didn't exist.

They were near the base of the hill now. This was where he had dropped *The Miraculous* yesterday.

But it was nowhere in sight.

He was turning in a slow circle, searching for it, when Faye interrupted him.

"What's up there?" She was pointing to the treeless Branch Hill. Her cloak caught the wind, making her look like some great bird. "A grave? That wasn't there the other day."

At the top of the hill, there was a shining spot, a glimmer that Wunder hadn't seen before.

"It can't be a grave," he told her. "There aren't any graves up there."

Faye didn't respond. She was already heading up the hill. Wunder followed her, trying not to think about his lost book, trying not to feel such a terrible weight in his stomach as he realized that it was gone, really gone.

They climbed the hill, Wunder gaining on Faye and her slow gait. As they neared the top, Wunder saw that the glimmer came from a stone, like a gravestone, with silver writing on it and carvings of flowers in the corners.

"It's that verse!" Faye had reached the stone. "'Behold! I tell you a miracle,'" she read aloud. "'We will not all sleep, but we will all be changed. Let us, then, change together. With great love, Milagros.'"

Wunder was right behind Faye, but now he stopped. He gaped at her. Then he gaped down at the stone.

The sun shone on it, like a spotlight, and the letters seemed to glow white-hot. The words were right there for him to see.

"Wundie. What's wrong?"

Faye had come over to him. She held on to his arm and peered into his eyes. Her bangs were pinned back.

Wunder pointed to the stone. "The verse," he said. His voice sounded high and thin now, like he had suddenly become smaller, shrunken. "Milagros."

Faye gripped his arm even tighter. "Yes. Who's Milagros?"

A cloud passed over the sun and the words stopped glowing. In fact, Wunder couldn't even make them out anymore. He squeezed his eyes closed. He blinked them open, hard. But the words were still a smudge of silver.

"My sister," he said. "My sister was named Milagros."

Chapter 12

Wunder sat on the ground next to Milagros's stone at the top of the branchless Branch Hill. He still felt dizzy and small and cold, even though the sun was back out. Faye sat cross-legged next to him, her magenta sweater hidden beneath her cloak.

"There are a number of possibilities," she was saying, her voice slow, contemplative. "Ghost is the most obvious and likely, I think."

"It's not obvious," Wunder said, "or likely."

"Your sister's spirit was not at rest for some reason, so she ordered herself a rock thing and put it here. If that's the case, maybe she's happy now."

"I've never heard of a ghost ordering itself a gravestone," Wunder said.

"Another possibility," Faye continued, "is that your sister has been reincarnated."

"When you're reincarnated, you get reborn right away," Wunder said. "So my sister would still be a newborn baby. How could a newborn baby order a gravestone?"

"Reincarnated and a time traveler, then," Faye said with a shrug. "You're not being very open here, Wundie."

Wunder frowned at her. "She wouldn't have the same name if she was reincarnated either. She'd be born to a totally new family with a totally new body. I don't think you know anything about reincarnation."

"I know some things," Faye replied, "but reincarnation is very complicated." Then her eyes widened. The smallest smile lifted the edges of her mouth. "Must be a zombie, then. I love zombies."

"My sister is not a zombie!" Wunder cried. "This isn't anything supernatural. This is—" He tried to think of an explanation, a rational explanation. "A coincidence. There must be more than one Milagros in Branch Hill."

"I've never heard that name before," Faye said.

Wunder traced the silver etching on the stone. "I chose it," he said quietly. He'd spent hours researching, tabbing name books from the library, compiling lists, saying each possibility aloud. When he finally found the right one, he'd known instantly. "It means miracles. Like my name." He stopped tracing the letters and put his hands in his lap. "Another explanation is that someone thought they were being nice—maybe someone my dad works with or my aunt Anita—and they had this memorial stone made as a—a tribute or something."

Faye gave a gloved-hand wave of dismissal. "You're really reaching, Wundie," she said. "I prefer my explanation. I know you were into happy, fuzzy-feeling phenomena, but I've always said there was something dark and malevolent about Branch Hill. Now we have a zombie and a witch." Then her eyes widened again and her mouth dropped open. "The witch!" she shrieked.

Wunder looked across the cemetery toward the woods. The tallest tower of the DoorWay House was visible over the tops of the gold-tipped trees. But with the sun in his eyes, he couldn't make out the spirals. The wood seemed black.

"What about her?"

"Come on, Wundie! Think about it!" Faye leaped to her feet. "This graveyard is practically in her backyard. She can't be some random woman who just happened to move into the DoorWay House right now. She must have something to do with it! What if she has everything to do with it? What if she can talk to the dead? What if she can raise the dead? Or what if—" Faye stopped pacing and leaned over him. Her cloak blocked the sun. "What if the witch *is* your sister?"

"That's ridiculous!" Wunder cried, his voice loud, louder than the thoughts that were now spinning through his head. "And even if it wasn't, it wouldn't make any sense. My sister was a baby, remember? Not an old woman."

"It's a miracle, Wundie," Faye said. "It doesn't have to make sense."

"It's a coincidence," Wunder replied angrily. "That's what miracles are! Coincidences. Or lies."

"You know you don't believe that, Wundie," Faye said.

"I do!" Wunder stood up. "Because it's the truth! Did you know—did you know that Thomas Jefferson made his own Bible? He cut out every single miracle, chopped them right out with scissors because he knew they were lies. And did you know that there's this principle—the law of truly large numbers—that says that with a big enough sample size, anything is possible? The things that seem like miracles are actually random events."

"I know about those things," Faye answered him, "because you talked about them at the Unexplainable and

75

Inexplicable Phenomenon Society meeting. And then you told us that there are all kinds of miracles and all kinds of ways to believe."

"Well, I don't think that anymore!" Wunder paced the hill. He no longer felt small or cold or dizzy. He just felt angry. "And I'm going to find out who put up the stone somehow, and it's going to be an ordinary person. And I'm going to tell them that they should take it down because even though it was a coincidence—even though they have the same name or they were trying to be sympathetic or whatever—it's upsetting people. And that's that."

Faye shook her head at him. "Rationality does not suit you, Wundie. But have it your way. We'll look up who ordered it."

"Look them up? Where?"

"Probably the town hall," Faye said. "This cemetery is owned by Branch Hill. My mom had to file all kinds of forms with them when my grandfather died."

"Fine!" Wunder started down the hill. "I'll go there now."

"It'll be closed soon. Tomorrow, Wundie. We'll go tomorrow afternoon."

"*I'll* go tomorrow afternoon," Wunder said.

"That's what I said, Wundie," Faye said. "We'll go tomorrow afternoon."

Chapter 13

Wunder told himself that all he was going to learn at the town hall was the name of the perfectly ordinary person who had put up the memorial stone. He told himself that it didn't have anything to do with ghosts or reincarnations or witches.

But even so, that night and the next day, he felt restless, edgy, unsettled. Like he was going somewhere he wasn't sure he was supposed to go. Like he might find something out that he didn't want to know.

After school, he hurried in the direction of the bike rack, where Faye was going to meet him. He was at the top of the school steps when he heard Tomás's voice.

"Hey, Wunder!" he called. "Wait up! I thought we could go to Oak Park. Play some soccer. What do you think?"

Wunder turned to see his best friends coming toward him. "Soccer?" This was another thing Tomás had started doing this year—asking to play soccer. Aside from a few halfhearted attempts at catch with his father—neither of them being particularly athletic—Wunder had never been interested in sports. He shook his head. "I can't. Sorry, Tomás."

"Or we could go to the Snack Shack," Tomás said. "Come on, Wunder. It's been me and Davy forever."

Davy had come up next to Tomás. "And what about the Unexplainable and Inexplicable Phenomenon Society?" he asked. "When are we going to have another meeting?"

"Never," Wunder said, louder and more forcefully than he had intended. Davy flinched. Wunder thought about apologizing or maybe explaining, but then he didn't.

Down at the bike rack, Faye had appeared. She held up one black-gloved hand.

"I have to go now," Wunder told his friends. "I have some things to do."

Tomás stared, goggle-eyed, at Faye. Her black cloak billowed. Her eyes were black smudges. "With *her*?"

"Yes," Wunder said. "With her."

He didn't say the rest of what he was thinking. He didn't say that Faye had asked him about his sister, that Faye knew his sister's name. He didn't think Tomás knew his sister's name. He didn't even think Davy did. He shoved his hands in his pockets and headed down the stairs.

"But, Wunder," Davy called after him, "I wanted to tell you something! It's about my paper route!"

Wunder used to help Davy with his deliveries on Sundays, when he had the most. They would take their bikes, cutting through the woods—which Davy would do only if Wunder was with him—talking about the latest miracles and tossing paper after paper.

"I can't help anymore, Davy," Wunder said.

He didn't turn back around.

Faye had brought her bike that day, so after she tied her cloak in a huge, velvety knot to keep it from getting caught in the wheels, they both rode to the town hall. Wunder stayed a little ahead the whole way so he wouldn't have to talk.

"I go to church here," Faye told him as they leaned their bikes against the rack next to the fountain.

"In the town hall? Is that allowed?" Wunder asked. "What about separation of church and state?"

"We rent a public meeting hall in the basement," Faye said. "It's a very small, exclusive church. You have to speak Korean to attend, so don't even ask. You're not invited."

Wunder's own church, St. Gerard's, was big and bright. There were high ceilings and stained-glass windows and polished pews that gleamed. He wasn't sure how he would feel about going to services in a basement.

"Not everyone needs somewhere fancy to pray," Faye told him. "My grandfather used to say he felt most spiritual walking in the woods. And I meditate in my room every morning."

"You do?"

"I do, Wundie," Faye said, wrapping her cloak tightly around herself. "My grandfather taught me that too. And it gives me serenity throughout my whole day. Don't I seem serene?"

She stared at him, eyes unblinking, face impassive. Wunder wasn't sure if it was a serene look necessarily.

"I guess," he said. "Maybe. Except when you scream."

"I'm only human, Wundie," Faye said. "Sometimes you have to scream."

They went through the double doors of the town hall. Inside, on the far wall, there was a mural of a long-limbed, green-leafed tree, and in front of it was a huge desk surrounded by rows of cabinets.

There was only one person at the desk. It was a woman who was wearing a shiny, bright pink shirt and glaring fiercely at her computer screen. Her gold name tag read EUGENIA. When she noticed them, Eugenia's bright pink mouth turned up in a sort of grimace-grin.

Wunder paused at the sight of that very unwelcoming expression, but Faye wandered right up to the desk.

That left Wunder no choice. Faye could not be trusted to talk to Eugenia alone.

"Hello, ma'am," he said, hurrying up to the desk. "I'm Wunder Ellis, and my friend and I had a question about a stone we found in the cemetery—not a grave marker, more like a memorial? Where would we find out about something like that?"

Eugenia had directed her grimace-grin at him while he spoke, but as soon as he was done, she focused her attention back on Faye. Faye stared right back, her face expressionless, her arms crossed under her black cloak.

"I'm sorry," Eugenia said, not sounding the least bit sorry, "but I really have work to do. Please see your little selves right out."

"Eugenia," Faye began. "Listen."

"I'm sure you're really busy!" Wunder hurried to cut her off. "We just want to know who bought the stone. Or asked the town to buy it, or however it's done."

Eugenia had already turned back to her computer screen. Her bright pink fingernails tap, tap, tapped sharply on the keyboard, dismissing them. "I'm so sorry, dear," she said, "but I can't give out that kind of information. Good-bye now."

"Why not, Eugenia? It's a public record, isn't it?" Faye asked, and Wunder noticed with some alarm that the sharpness had already started to creep into her voice.

"Well, I don't know if it's public per se," Eugenia replied, "but I do know that it certainly is *not* public to two little children, especially when one of them is dressed like some kind of Frankenstein bat creature."

"Thank you for your time, ma'am," Wunder said. It was very obvious to him that they were going to have to figure out another way to get what they had come for. "Let's go, Faye."

"Public information is public information." Faye's voice was even louder, faster, shriller. "You have no right to keep it from us."

Eugenia looked back up from her computer. Her

grimace-grin had become a scowl. "Here's some public information for you: Graveyards are not playgrounds. It seems to me that you and your friend Mr. Ellis have an unhealthy obsession with death, and I certainly will not be contributing to that."

"You are discriminating against me!" Faye screeched.

"You lower your voice, young lady," Eugenia said.

"You are making judgments about my character and my life choices based on my outward appearance! Based on my clothing!"

"Of course I am," Eugenia snapped. "What are you thinking, dressing like that? And that eyeliner. You look absolutely ridiculous!"

Faye smacked a gloved hand onto Eugenia's desk, her ridiculously lined eyes blazing. "Here's some public information for *you*—we are trying to uncover a very significant miracle. A possible resurrection! And you—you don't know anything about miracles. You don't know anything about mystery. You don't know anything about cloaks! Et cetera!"

"Come on, Faye," Wunder said. "Let's just go."

Eugenia had gotten to her feet. Her hands were on her hips, and she was emitting bright pink waves of fury. "What I *do* know is that you two better show your little selves out of this town hall before I have to call security and have you escorted from the premises!" She jabbed one pink-nailed finger in Faye's direction. "You need someone to get you in line. And you need to get to know the Lord!"

"I already know the Lord," Faye replied. "And if you really knew anything about Him, you'd know that He likes miracles too. And probably cloaks! Robes, for sure!"

"Faye, come *on*!" Wunder managed to pull Faye toward the door by the much-discussed cloak. He yanked her outside, into the late-afternoon sun.

"Can you believe that woman?" Faye cried, stomping past the fountain. "She's supposed to be a public servant. And a Frankenstein bat? That doesn't even make sense!"

"You are wearing black gloves. And a cape—I mean, cloak."

"I'm a student of the paranormal!" Faye yelled. Then she flipped her hood over her head.

She was under there for quite a while, but when she came out, her face had relaxed into its usual deadpan expression. "I guess we know what we have to do," she said.

"We do?"

"Break in," Faye said. "Steal the record."

Wunder shook his head. "No, Faye. We can't do that."

No matter what he believed or didn't believe, the law still mattered. Breaking and entering would never be okay.

"Wundie. Listen," Faye said. "You want to figure out who put that memorial stone there, right? If it's someone with the same name as your sister or someone doing it in honor of your sister or—"

Wunder didn't want her to say the other possibility again. "Yes, I do!" he cried. "But we'll get caught. We'll get in trouble."

"We won't," Faye said. "Because I have a plan. And if we do get caught"—she raised her voice to a scream again—"I will place the blame squarely on the shoulders of Eugenia the Pink Priss!"

Chapter 14

Wunder had always marveled at kids who snuck out of their houses in movies. They made it seem so easy— opening their unsqueaky windows, shimmying down very sturdy drainpipes. He never thought he would be brave enough to do something like that. He was sure if he tried, he would be caught.

But on Saturday at midnight, he crept out of his room, left through the front door, and biked off down the street.

No one noticed.

Faye was waiting for him at the corner a few blocks away. She stood in a bright circle of streetlamp light, making it look like she was about to be abducted by aliens. Or like she had just been zapped down to earth.

"Wundie, turn that flashlight off," she said as he rode up.

"We need it," Wunder said. "How else will we see where we're going?"

"There are streetlights some of the way," Faye said. "And there's the moon, the stars, et cetera. We're going to break into a government building, Wundie. We need to be discreet."

"Discreet like you were with Eugenia?"

"I'm sorry, what was that, Wundie? I can't hear you when you mumble," Faye said.

Wunder turned off the flashlight with a sigh and stuck it into his backpack.

But as they pedaled off, he wished he had kept it out. The darkness was so dark that he didn't understand how Faye could see where she was going. He rode behind her, concentrating on the little red reflector on the back of her bike.

He knew that in another time, in different circumstances, this would be an adventure—riding his bike in near-total darkness while everyone was asleep, stars burning bright, bright above, sharp autumn air waking him up again and again.

But it wasn't another time. It was now, and he was going to break into the town hall to prove that a stone in a cemetery wasn't a miracle.

And not just that. Wunder knew that what he was really proving to himself was that none of it—the witch, the bird, the DoorWay House—none of it was a miracle. After tonight, he wouldn't have to force himself not to think about those things, because he would know that they meant nothing.

After tonight, the stone of his heart would never warm again.

They rode their bikes to the back of the town hall and hid them in the bushes. Then Faye led him down a small flight of stairs to a basement door.

"How are we going to get in?" he whispered.

He had to wait for his answer while Faye slowly pinned back her bangs, then searched through the many pockets of her voluminous cloak. Finally, she held up a silver key. "My mom's been setting up the chairs for church every Saturday afternoon since before I was born," she said. "So she has her own key. Take that, Eugenia the Pink Priss!"

Inside, the basement was filled with rows of folding chairs. Each chair had a blue book and a red book set on its seat. There was a podium at the front of the room, the plain wooden kind that teachers use, and a small table draped in green cloth with a cross set on top of it.

Even though the room didn't look anything like St. Gerard's, Wunder could feel that it was a special place for the people who met there. He moved slowly and quietly down the center aisle.

Faye, for all her supernatural sensitivity, didn't appear to feel the same way. She was already at the other end of the room, opening a metal door set to the left of the podium. There was a staircase there.

"Up we go," she said, and Wunder hurried over to her.

They crept up the stairs, their footsteps only slightly muffled by the blue industrial carpet. At the top, there was another door. It was just like the door at the bottom— metal, beige-painted, and completely plain—no windows, no signs.

"I don't know if my key opens this one," Faye said. "I guess we'll see."

She pushed the key into the doorknob and turned. The lock clicked open. She turned the knob, pushed, and—

BLEEEEEEP! BLEEEEEEP! BLEEEEEEP!

"Wundie! Listen!" Faye shrieked.

Wunder froze at the sound of the alarm, his heart pounding, his eyes wide. They were going to be caught. And even worse than that—they weren't going to find out what they had come to find out. He wasn't going to prove anything. He was going to be left wondering and wondering and wondering.

He couldn't let that happen.

"Hurry!" he shouted.

The alarm bleeped on as they raced through the doorway and into the main foyer of the town hall. There was Eugenia's desk ahead of them, computer screen black, cabinets rising up behind like sentries.

Wunder yanked open desk drawers while Faye rummaged through cabinets. He tried to be careful, but his heart was beating so fast and his hands seemed clumsy and strange. Papers and paper clips and sticky notes were soon scattered across the floor.

And then, there it was. A black three-ring binder with the words CEMETERY RECORDS typed in black on a white label.

"I found it!" Wunder cried. He flipped the binder open to the middle, but inside was row after row after row of dates and names, and the alarm was still blaring. He wasn't going to be able to find the right record fast enough.

He slammed the binder shut and tucked it under his arm. "Let's go!"

They went out the way they'd come in, pounding down the stairs, through the meeting room, and out the basement door. They leaped onto their bicycles and pedaled away as fast as they could, Wunder balancing the binder on his handlebars.

But instead of getting far, far away from the scene of the crime, Faye jerked her bike into the first alley they came to, less than a block from the town hall.

"Let me see," she said, propping her bike against the wall.

"We can't stop now," Wunder said. He could still hear the sound of the alarm from there. "They might find us. What about discretion?"

But he got off his bike too and sat on the ground. He pulled his flashlight from his backpack.

He opened to the first page of the binder. The entries turned out to be in chronological order, but the most recent one was more than three months old. There were some loose papers though, in the front folder of the binder. Wunder pulled out the first one.

The paper was creased in thirds. When Wunder unfolded it, he saw that it was a form stamped with the oak leaf seal of the town of Branch Hill. Across the top, it read MEMORIAL OTHER THAN GRAVESTONE.

"What did you find?" Faye peered over his shoulder. Her cloak fell across the paper.

"I'm looking," Wunder said. "Back up a little, would you?"

She moved back about two inches.

INSCRIPTION, the form read. And then, in sprawling black script: *"Behold! I tell you a miracle. We will not all sleep, but*

91

we will all be changed." Let us, then, change together. With great love, Milagros.

Faye reached for the binder. "Let me see. You're taking forever."

Wunder tightened his grip. "I'm. Looking. Hold. On."

DEDICATOR, the form read. And beneath that, in the same rambling lettering, there were three words. Not a name. Just: *The DoorWay House.*

Wunder stared at the words lit up by his flashlight. He could imagine the hand that had written those words, the same hand that had waved to him on the day of his sister's funeral.

"It says 'The DoorWay House,'" he told Faye very, very quietly.

"'The DoorWay House'?" She leaned over to see the paper. "'The DoorWay House'? What do you mean 'The DoorWay House'?"

"That's who ordered the stone," Wunder said. "The DoorWay House."

Faye pressed her hands against her cheeks. "The witch," she breathed.

The alarm suddenly stopped.

"The witch," Wunder said. He put the form back in the binder. Then he set the binder on the ground and got onto his bicycle.

"I'm leaving now," he said. "I'm going home."

"You're leaving the binder here?"

"We broke into the town hall," Wunder said. "I don't think we should keep the evidence."

Faye considered this, then nodded. "That makes sense. But what do we do now? We know it's the witch. But why did she do it? What does she want? What does she have to do with your sister? We have to go see her."

Wunder shook his head as he pressed his foot onto the pedal. He had been so sure that finding out who ordered the memorial stone would make him less confused. Instead, he had a whole new set of questions, and he didn't want to think about any of them, especially Faye's last one.

"No, Faye," he said. "I don't want to see her. I don't believe in witches."

But his words sounded, even to his own ears, far from convincing.

He had a dream that night.

He was at the funeral again, listening to the minister yelling on and on. His father was next to him, crying and crying. In front of them was the white coffin.

Then the lid of the coffin opened.

And out of it climbed the witch.

The autumn wind blew, hard and strong. The witch spread her arms out. Her black hair fanned out from her head, and the strips of her white clothing lifted, flapped, like wings. She rose up in the air, and she let out a *caw*, like a bird.

But there were words in the *caw* too.

"'Behold! I tell you a miracle'!" she cawed. "A miracle! A miracle!"

Part Three

THE WITCH

Chapter 15

When Wunder arrived at school on Monday morning, Faye was standing at his locker. She didn't say *Good morning* or *How was your Sunday?* or anything like that. Instead, she said, "We have to go to the DoorWay House. Today."

"I don't want to go," Wunder said.

After waking up from his dream on the night of the break-in, Wunder hadn't been able to get back to sleep. The crib-bar shadows had reached his face, covered his mouth and his eyes, crept up the sides of the wall next to him, and still he had not slept.

The next morning, his father had knocked on his door. "Time to get up, Wunder," he had called. "And hurry—we're going to be late for church."

Wunder had gone to his door and opened it. "I'm not going," he had said, before he had really thought about what it would mean to say this.

But once he'd said it, he hadn't changed his mind, even though his father had been confused, then upset, then angry.

Finally, after his father had said very loudly, "We go together every week, and this week is no different. You have to go with me, and that's that!" Wunder's mother had come out of her room and into the hall where they were arguing.

She had looked exhausted, like she had on the soup night, but Wunder knew it was a good sign that she was coming out of her room. And he knew that she would understand, she would explain to his father that things had changed.

And she had. "If Wunder doesn't want to go," she had said, "then he doesn't have to."

But his father had said, "Yes, he does. Wunder isn't allowed to give up on everything like you."

He had started apologizing almost immediately, but Wunder's mother had gone back into the room, shut the door, and locked it. Wunder's father had stood there for a long time, trying to get her to come out again. But she hadn't.

Finally, he had left. Alone.

And standing by his locker now at school, Wunder had realized that there was no reason to go to the DoorWay House, no need to keep asking questions. He had his answers.

Things were getting worse, not better. Things were falling apart. His house used to be filled with love, but it seemed like that love was being washed away, was being buried, deeper and deeper every day.

"Listen, Wundie—" Faye began.

"I don't want to go!" Wunder cried.

But, of course, Faye was waiting next to his bicycle that afternoon.

"I'm just here for another one of our walks," she said. "Just walking. No witch talk."

Wunder sighed. "You've said that before."

"I mean it this time."

"I doubt it," Wunder said. But he went with her anyway.

It took only a few minutes of walking for Faye to break her promise.

"I know why you don't want to go to the DoorWay House," she said.

"Just walking," Wunder reminded her.

"I lied," Faye said. "Remember the first meeting of the Unexplainable and Inexplicable Phenomenon Society?"

Wunder sighed. "Of course I do." It had been only four weeks ago, although it felt like much, much longer.

"Remember what you said at the end?" She pasted a huge grin on her face and stuck her hands into the pockets of her pastel-green-and-blue sweater dress. "'To me, every hour of the light and dark is a miracle . . . unspeakably perfect miracles'!"

"I was quoting Walt Whitman," Wunder said. "And I don't smile like that."

"Well, not now you don't," Faye said. "But that is a very accurate imitation of the way you smiled before." She took her hands out of her pockets. "Like you really meant it."

"I meant it then," Wunder told her. "But I didn't know then what I know now."

Faye fixed her unblinking stare on him. "You didn't mean it then," she said. "You only thought you did because nothing bad had ever happened to you before. And now something bad has happened."

Wunder waited to answer her as they passed the town hall. He didn't see any police officers around, but he felt nervous anyway.

100

"I've had bad things happen to me before," he said once they were a safe distance away.

"Like what?" Faye asked.

"My grandmother died."

"That *is* sad," Faye said. "Did you know her well?"

"No," Wunder admitted. "She died right after I was born." He thought for a moment, hands in his pockets. "I broke my arm when I was five. That's how I met Tomás. In the emergency room. He'd broken his arm too. I thought it was a miracle at the time." It was in *The Miraculous*, Entry #97.

"That must have hurt," Faye said. "But I bet your mom held your hand and then you got ice cream or something. I bet you've never had anything really bad happen to you until now. That's why you believed in miracles before and now you don't."

Wunder frowned at her. "Well, then, I guess you've never had anything bad happen to you, since you believe in all kinds of stuff."

"Oh no, I have," Faye said. "Don't you remember my grandfather died?" She waved her hand through the air. "And my dad left when I was little. And my mother thinks I'm a weirdo. So does my sister, Grace."

In Wunder's opinion, Faye *was* kind of a weirdo. But he

also knew that some people probably thought he was too. Miracology was not exactly a typical childhood pastime.

His parents hadn't seemed to think he was weird though. They had bought him *The Miraculous*. They had read every entry, searched through old newspapers with him, bought him books, driven him to the sites of local phenomena. Back when he had believed in miracles, he had been sure that his parents would always be there, listening to him and supporting him. Loving him.

But now everything had changed. If his sister's death was the worst thing that had ever happened to him, his parents' grief was a close second. He wasn't sure of anything anymore.

"Then why do you believe in that stuff?" he asked Faye. "Witches and werewolves and zombies?"

Faye stopped midstep to pin her bangs back. Wunder waited for her, although he wished he hadn't when she finished and stepped very close to him.

"Because I know enough to know that I don't know everything," Faye said, staring into his eyes. "I know you liked your sunshine-and-sparkles miracles, Wundie, the ones where the bad thing doesn't happen, where life is always perfect. But sometimes the bad thing does happen. People hurt your feelings and disappoint you. People die."

She was silent for a moment. Wunder thought she would flip up her hood, but then she took a deep breath and continued. "But sometimes the brightest miracles are hidden in the darkest moments." She nodded, almost to herself. "That's right. But you have to search for them. You can't be afraid of the dark."

Then she unpinned her bangs and started walking again.

"I'm not afraid," Wunder said when he caught up to her. "I just don't believe in miracles anymore."

He was thinking about Faye's words though, thinking about the light and the dark as they entered the woods where the color was creeping up the green of the leaves, taking them over, bit by bit. Wunder hadn't even realized they were going that way, but of course they were. And now that they were there, he felt himself speeding up, moving faster. Soon they were at the head of the dirt trail where the live oak and the resurrection fern were as green as ever.

And there she was. He could see her through the branches, sitting on the porch. The spiraling house rose up behind her, crooked and crumbling. The spiraled chair rocked back and forth, back and forth. The newspaper flutter, fluttered on her lap.

She saw them right away, almost like she had been waiting for them. She waved.

And then she stood up and she beckoned.

"Do you think we should go over there?" Faye asked out of the side of her mouth.

And Wunder knew what he had said. There was no reason to talk to her. She was just an old woman. Nothing she could say would make anything better.

But he was also still thinking about what Faye had said. He was thinking about the darkness in his house, the darkness inside of him. And he was wondering if she could possibly be right about the miracles hidden there. Maybe that was why he still had so many questions. Maybe that was why he kept coming here, day after day.

And so, as he stared at the witch waving them toward her, he found himself saying, "Maybe. I guess. I mean, of course. Of course we should. To ask about the memorial stone. Just about that though. Nothing else."

Next to him, Faye pulled her hood over her head. He heard her swinging her cloak around herself, the black material swooshing as it cocooned her completely. "Okay," she said, her voice muffled by a layer of velvet. "But follow my lead. You don't know about witches. I do."

"She's not a witch," Wunder said.

"Wundie. Listen," Faye said. "You're the miracle expert.

When someone turns water into wine, I'll ask your opinion. But I'm a student of the paranormal. When a mysterious ancient woman wearing a robe summons children to a haunted house, you should listen to me. Now let's go."

Chapter 16

For years, Wunder had passed by the DoorWay House going to and from school. For years, he had peered through the vines and leaves and branches at its towers and windows. For years, he had watched the spirals.

But in all that time, he had never climbed the DoorWay House's steps. He had never touched its wood. He had never peeked in its windows. He had always felt it was a place that could not be disturbed, a sacred place.

Up close for the first time, he found that the house's wood wasn't smooth, the way it appeared from a distance. Up close, it was splintered and peeling, rough and unfinished looking.

And up close, the witch was like the house. She had more wrinkles than Wunder had ever seen. It was as if her skin was a paper bag that had been crumpled into the tiniest possible ball, then spread back out. Her hair, however, was long and thick and pure black.

As they mounted the steps, Wunder met the witch's gaze. Her eyes were so dark that he couldn't even see her pupils, and they reminded him of someone. He looked away, back at the house.

"DoorWay Tree wood," the witch said. Her voice was scratchy and very soft. It sounded like it was coming from far away.

"What?"

"The house." She gestured behind her. "It's made of wood from the *Arbor liminis*. The DoorWay Tree."

She was staring at him, but Wunder focused on the house. He followed the curve of the spiral closest to him with his eyes. It was a perfect, perfect circle. "I saw it spinning once," he said.

Next to him, Faye yanked the hood off her head and turned to him, shocked.

The witch nodded slowly. "It can look like that," she said. Then she smiled. "Come inside. Come and have tea with me, Wunder."

Now Faye let out a shriek.

"You too, Faye," the witch said. Faye shrieked again. "I haven't had any visitors in this house yet. But I have wanted them."

"Tea?" Wunder said. "Maybe. I guess. Sure. Sure, we can have some tea."

As soon as the witch turned around, Faye leaned toward him.

"She knows our names!" she whispered. "Don't eat or drink anything. That's how witches capture unsuspecting children. And you never told me you'd seen the spirals spin too!"

The door swung open. The witch went inside. Faye grabbed Wunder's hand, and Wunder didn't try to stop her. They entered the house together.

As soon as Wunder crossed the threshold, it happened. The stone of his heart—the stone that had only barely warmed since his sister's death—began to shiver. The stone of his heart began to shake.

Wunder wrapped the hand not holding Faye's around the side of his chest. He held on tightly.

They were standing in a long dimly lit hall. There were doors on either side, doors with tarnished gold knobs and keyholes. Even here, inside the house, the wood was spiraled. The floors, the walls, the ceilings—every visible surface. It gave the place a jumbled-up look, a distorted look, so that Wunder felt like he might topple over if he moved too fast.

"There are not many DoorWay Trees left in the world," the witch said. She moved gracefully down the hallway, far more easily than Wunder would have expected for someone her age. She seemed unaffected by the spirals. "And even fewer houses made of them. Houses, of course, are temporary places. But the trees—the trees can last forever. Very deep roots, very high branches."

"Are they magical?" Faye asked. Her voice was shrill. "What do they do? Are you magical? What do you do?"

"Magical? I don't know about magical." The witch made a small noise in her throat that might have been a laugh. "But the trees are special. Yes, yes, yes, so special. All around the world, all throughout history, they have been there. There was one here once, in Branch Hill. But no more. There are fewer and fewer. Most of us have forgotten them."

"I've never seen wood like this anywhere else," Wunder said. He released his grip on himself long enough to brush his fingers against the spirals on the wall.

"The closest one is not close enough," the witch replied.

"I believe that every town should have a DoorWay Tree. But, of course, that is not up to me."

"Who is it up to?" Faye asked. "The high priestess of your coven?"

The witch didn't answer, but she made the maybe-laugh again.

The hallway opened onto a large parlor. Everything in the room was coated in a thick layer of dust. There was a black piano and a soot-blackened fireplace. The walls were covered in shelves, but the shelves were empty.

Wunder wanted to ask a thousand questions. He wanted to ask if anyone had ever lived there before and why the spirals spun. He wanted to ask why she was there and if her name was Milagros and if she had ordered the memorial stone. But his thoughts were coming so fast and his heart was shaking so violently that all he could manage to say was, "You just moved in?"

"Ah, yes, yes, yes," the witch said. "I arrived very recently. Although I doubt I'll be able to stay long."

Through the parlor they went and then through a dining room filled with a long spiral-wood table. A chandelier topped with melted candles hung above, swinging slightly in an unfelt draft.

Then they entered a small, cluttered kitchen at the very

back of the house. Well-worn copper pots and tinted glass jars and what seemed like a hundred teacups littered the counters. The appliances were faded and old-fashioned.

"Have a seat," the witch said, gesturing toward a little table in the kitchen's center. "I will make some tea for us. There is no milk, but there may be sugar."

She began opening cabinets. Each one squeaked as if it had not been touched in years. Wunder found a rusty stool and sat down. He couldn't tell if the kitchen table was made of DoorWay Tree wood because it was completely hidden. Newspapers were spread everywhere.

Faye sat next to him on a paint-flecked wooden chair.

"Remember," she hissed. "Don't drink anything. Pretend if you have to."

"She's not a witch," Wunder whispered back.

But he wasn't so sure. He was less sure now than ever. He watched as the witch found an iron teakettle and filled it with water from the tap. He watched as she lit the gas stove with a long red-tipped match and then set the kettle on the flames. Her movements were easy and fluid. It was if she were two people at once: the old woman with the wrinkled face, and someone else, someone young with long black hair and strong limbs.

And with every passing second, it seemed more and

more likely that the stone of his heart was going to split wide open. He had let go of Faye's hand, but he was still clutching his own side so tightly that his fingertips were tingling. Everything seemed fuzzy and out of focus, like a dream.

"Wunder," Faye whispered, interrupting his thoughts. "Look down."

Wunder looked down at the table.

And right into his sister's face.

Chapter 17

The newspaper on the table was open to Milagros's obituary. Wunder's father had put it in the paper the day before her funeral, although Wunder's mother had not wanted him to do that either. In the picture, Milagros was wearing the little white knit cap that they had given her at the hospital. She was surrounded by tubes and wires, and she was looking at the camera with serious eyes, black eyes.

"They're all open to the obituaries," Faye whispered to him.

"The tea is almost ready," the witch said from the counter where she was selecting teacups. "And I have much to talk about with you two. Yes, yes, yes. There is much to discuss."

Wunder looked from his sister's eyes to the other newspapers. More faces gazed up at him. Family pictures and individual portraits, a man in a military uniform, a young woman smiling in front of a red-roofed house. Faye was right. They were all obituaries.

"I have to go," Wunder said. "We have to go."

He stood up. Faye stood up too.

"I see," the old woman said. She was holding two teacups, one in each hand. "But you will return? I would like for you to return. Both of you."

"Maybe," Wunder said. He edged toward the kitchen door. "I guess. Sure. We'll come back. We just have to go now."

The old woman started forward. "Before you leave," she said, "I have something for you." She set the teacups on the kitchen table, shifted around some of the newspapers, and then held something up.

Something black with white letters.

The Miraculous.

"I think you lost this," she said.

Wunder took the book, wordless, wide-eyed.

"And I also wondered," the witch said, "if you would

do me a favor." She reached into the folds of her white clothing and pulled out an envelope. "Would you deliver this for me?"

She held it out to Wunder.

"'Deliver this,'" Wunder echoed. "Sure. I can do that." But he didn't take the envelope. He kept his grip on *The Miraculous*.

"What is it?" Faye asked, her voice high and tight.

"It's . . . an invitation," the witch said.

"For what? A party?"

"A party? I suppose it will be a party of sorts," the witch said. "But also something else." She leaned closer to them. She smelled like the woods. "You will see. I have letters for both of you too. When you are ready for them."

Her black eyes gleamed. And Wunder stared back, stared into those eyes—until Faye jabbed him in the side.

Then he grabbed the envelope, shoved it into his pocket, and ran.

He ran through the dining room where the chandelier swung ever so slightly and through the parlor with its vacant shelves and through the long fun-house-mirror hallway.

For a moment, the front doorknob wouldn't turn under his sweat-slippery hand, and panic rose up in him. But then it did and the door opened and he flung himself through it and into the brightness of the outside.

Faye was right behind him. She slammed the door shut, and as she did there was the sudden sound of spinning.

But the sound came from the path ahead, not from the house behind. Through the trees, Wunder could see a head of curly dark hair and a neon-green bicycle zooming away.

"What was that?" Faye gasped. "What's going on?"

"Davy, I think," Wunder replied. "He must have followed us."

They hurried down the dirt trail, then onto the path, where the woods pulled them in. The cool breeze blew over them, the green light—now tinted, tainted as the leaves turned—washed over them. Wunder wondered why Davy had come there; he was terrified of the woods. The only time he ever ventured in was when Wunder helped him on his Sunday paper route.

Then Wunder stopped thinking about Davy. Because there were far more pressing issues at hand.

"Now we know for sure that she is a witch or"—Faye gave him a sideways look—"or someone else."

Wunder started to say what he always said, that she was just an old woman, but then he stopped.

"Don't tell me you didn't feel what I felt in that house," Faye said.

Wunder wiggled the fingers of the hand that had been clutching his side. He let his breathing slow as his heart grew stiller and stiller.

And he listened as above them a bird cawed and cawed and cawed.

"I don't know what I feel," he said.

Chapter 18

When Wunder turned onto his street, the first thing he saw was flashing light. Red-and-blue flashing light. There was a police car in front of his house.

Officer Soto was sitting in the living room. Officer Soto was Tomás's dad. He was one of three police officers in Branch Hill, so Wunder had figured that if the police were called about the town hall break-in, Officer Soto would know about it. But he hadn't expected to see him at his house.

Wunder's mother was in the chair across from him. Neither of them was speaking, even though they had known each other for years.

"Oh, hey, Wunder." Officer Soto jumped to his feet as Wunder entered. He looked relieved. "You're here."

"Hi, Officer Soto," Wunder said. He put his hands in his pockets. His heart was pounding. "How are you? How's Tomás? Everything okay?"

"I'm fine, Tomás is fine." Officer Soto cracked his knuckles. "But actually, everything's not okay."

"Officer Soto says you broke into the town hall, Wunder."

Officer Soto and Wunder both turned to look at Wunder's mother. She was still sitting, and she was still staring across the room. It was almost as if she hadn't spoken.

"Well," Officer Soto said, "I said we think it was him. The clerk, Ms. Eugenia Simone, she says someone who claimed he was you was in there the day before with a"—he consulted the small notebook he was carrying—"'foul-tempered, profanely garbed vampire girl.' Says the two asked to see a particular set of records, which she refused to let them see. And now those records are missing . . ."

Officer Soto waited for Wunder to respond, but not for very long. "Things being what they are," he continued, "circumstances being a certain way—if we got those records back, the whole thing could just be over and done with. Papers go missing every day, no big deal. So . . ."

He cracked his knuckles again, loud, painful-sounding

119

pops. Wunder tried frantically to think of what to say. But what *could* he say? He had broken into the town hall. He had taken the cemetery records. And he had never been any good at lying.

"Well, you let me know if you think of anything, Wunder," the officer finally said. He nodded at Wunder's mother. "Mrs. Ellis."

Then he walked out the front door.

Wunder waited, uncertain, conflicted. His mother stayed in the chair. More than anything, what he wanted right then was for her to look at him, to tell him what to do. She had always helped him figure things out.

But she didn't look at him. The way she was sitting there, she might as well have been a stranger. She might as well have been someone who had nothing to do with him, some-one who wasn't connected to him at all.

Then she said, "I'm sorry, Wunder, but I'm not sure I can handle this." She turned to him finally, and her eyes were red. "It's hard to—this is a lot for me right now."

Now Wunder knew what his father had felt like yesterday, knocking on the door and apologizing to his mother. He couldn't remember ever making her cry before. It was a horrible feeling. "You don't have to worry," he said. "Every-thing's fine."

Then he ran outside.

"Officer Soto!" he called. "When I was walking home—I saw—in an alley near the town hall. There was a binder there. Maybe—maybe that's what you're looking for."

Officer Soto studied him for a minute, his brow furrowed. He looked like he was going to say something, but not something angry. Then he nodded.

"Okay, Wunder," he said. "I'll check it out. Thanks for letting me know."

When Wunder came back into the house, his mother was gone. His parents' door was shut.

Chapter 19

That night Wunder sat at his desk in his bare room and tried to sort through what had happened that day. Everything was so jumbled though, so twisted and distorted, like the hallway of the DoorWay House.

There were no answers.

Just questions, more and more questions.

Why did the witch have *The Miraculous*? Why had she been looking at the obituaries? Why had she ordered the cemetery stone?

And other questions, questions that had to do with the way the DoorWay House made him feel and how the witch's eyes reminded him of his sister.

"Now I have a black-eyed baby," his mother had whispered to him on the night his sister was born, "to go with my blue-eyed baby." She had hugged him tight there in the hospital room as they stood watch over Milagros's incubator, as they watched her sleep in a nest of wires and tubes, both still believing that a miracle was on its way no matter what the doctors said.

Wunder jumped out of his chair and paced his room. He should never have gone to the DoorWay House. He should never have broken into the town hall. He had hurt his mother even more and for what? Questions with no answers.

He shoved his hands into his pockets—and there it was. An answer.

The envelope from the witch.

The envelope was cream-colored with darker, discolored edges, as if it had sat somewhere for a long time. It was held shut by a wax seal. The wax was black and imprinted with the shape of a tree, a mostly bare tree with deep, spread-out roots and a few flowers on its long-reaching limbs.

Wunder ran his fingers over the seal, tracing from roots to branches and back again. Then he turned the envelope over.

On the other side there was a name written in black sprawling script:

Branch Hill was a small town, but it was big enough that the average resident couldn't possibly know everyone. But Wunder was a former miracologist. He had spent countless hours reading the local newspaper and gathering stories from his neighbors. They had written him letters, agreed to interviews, called him on the phone.

He didn't know everyone in Branch Hill. But he knew their miracles.

And, of course, he had kept track of them all.

Wunder pulled *The Miraculous* out of his backpack. The book's familiar worn cover looked even more worn now. There was dirt caked over the white lettering and the silver edges were crushed in places.

He carried the book to his bed, where he opened to the first page—Entry #1—and began to flip through.

The miracles passed before his eyes. A news story from Colorado of a three-year-old girl found alive in the woods five days after she went missing. A letter from his neighbor Susan Holt telling him about the starling who had sung her to sleep every night since she was a little girl, even following her when she moved across town. An anecdote about the philosopher-poet Rumi silencing some impertinent frogs copied from a book his mother had given him.

An entry about Davy's mother and how the doctors had told her that her tumor was shrinking.

And then there it was—a clipping from his church's bulletin and then his own words. It read like this:

Miraculous Entry #603

PRAISES THIS WEEK FROM ST. GERARD'S:
Luis Aritza
Florence Dabrowski
Edith Greenwald
Robert Ozols

Every week for a long time Florence Dabrowski has been listed in the Prayer Requests section of the bulletin. And then at church today I saw her name again—but it wasn't in the Prayer Requests section. It was in the Praises section. She must have gotten better!

It wasn't Sylvester, but it was something. Florence Dabrowski went to his church.

And she was a miracle.

What did the witch want with Sylvester, the other Dabrowski? Did it have something to do with Florence?

The answer was there, right there in his hands. The answer to those questions and maybe others.

But Wunder didn't open the envelope.

He didn't want to know. He didn't want to look for the bright in the dark. He would just throw the letter away, along with *The Miraculous*.

But he didn't.

He put *The Miraculous* in his backpack.

And he put the letter on his nightstand.

He had another dream that night.

He was holding the envelope in his hand when the tree on the wax seal began to grow. Its branches spread up and out, through the ceiling. Its roots reached the floor and tunneled down, into the floorboards. The tree grew and grew until it was enormous, wider than his house, taller than the tallest tower of the DoorWay House.

And covering it, round and perfect and bright, were the spirals. It was a DoorWay Tree. And on the very top branch, half-hidden behind white flowers, was the old woman.

"'We will all be changed!'" she cawed from her perch. "Changed! Changed!"

Chapter 20

Wunder put the letter in his pocket the next morning.
Then he took his time getting ready. He wanted to be late
because he was worried about the questions that would be
waiting for him at school. Because by now Tomás would
probably know about the town hall break-in.

And he did. When Wunder slipped into his seat in first
period English right before the bell rang, Tomás swung
around to face him.

"Wunder!" he whispered. "What's going on?"

But then Mr. Groves—who was known for giving deten-
tions for even the slightest infractions, like sneezing without
covering your nose—started taking roll. Tomás frowned,
flipped his hair, and turned back around.

At the end of class, Wunder rushed from the room while everyone was still packing up. He saw Davy watching him leave, front teeth chewing on his lip. He thought about asking what Davy had been doing in the woods, but then he didn't. It would be easier to avoid him.

All day, he dodged his old friends. He ate lunch in the stairwell, then told Ms. Shunem he had a stomachache and needed to go see the school nurse, because her science class was small and informal and Tomás would have plenty of time to talk to him there. When the last bell rang, Wunder was relieved that he had made it through the day without having to explain himself to anyone—

But Tomás was waiting for him at his locker. And when Wunder tried to walk right past, Tomás stepped in front of him.

"So did you really do it?" he asked.

"Do what?" Wunder went to his locker and focused on spinning the combination dial.

"You know what," Tomás said.

"Your dad isn't supposed to talk about police stuff with you," Wunder said. He pulled his earth sciences book out, put his English composition book back in. "It's confidential. That's the law."

Tomás snorted. Wunder wasn't looking at him, but he

was almost sure he could hear the sound of hair being flipped.

"Come on, Wunder," Tomás said. "If I robbed the town hall and your dad knew about it, you'd know about it too. My dad thought I might have been with you. I almost got in serious trouble!" Wunder didn't say anything. He knelt to shove his books into his backpack. "Hello? Wunder? Aren't you going to say anything?"

"I'm sorry you almost got in trouble," Wunder said.

Tomás snorted again, but this time more forcefully. "That's it? That's all you're going to say?"

Davy came up then. "Wunder, I heard—" He stammered to a stop, blinking back and forth between Tomás, who had his arms raised in disbelief, and Wunder, who had stood and was glaring at his friend. "Snack Shack?" he finally squeaked.

"All *I'm* going to say?" Wunder said. "Me? I'm not the one who doesn't want to talk about anything!"

"What's that supposed to mean?" Tomás demanded. "I've been at your locker every day, and I'm always asking you to hang out, even though you hardly talk now and you never smile and you don't want to go anywhere. It's not like I don't have better things to do! It's not like I don't have other friends!"

Wunder reeled at these words—but because Tomás was right. They always used to meet at Tomás's locker, never his. And Tomás *had* been asking him to do things. Wunder's anger started to die down.

Then, with one thought, it flared up again. "That may be true, but you haven't said anything—not one thing—about my sister. You haven't mentioned her once, neither of you! You're both just pretending like nothing happened!"

"What are we supposed to say?" Tomás cried. "If you wanted to talk about it, you should have brought it up. And anyway, it's not like it was your dad or someone you really knew. She was alive for what—a day? Two days? What's the big deal?"

It seemed like the hallway went silent after these words. If there was noise, Wunder couldn't hear it. All he could hear was the sound of his blood rushing past his ears and the sound of his own breathing, fast and tight. He saw Davy's face, hands pressed to his mouth, aghast.

"Eight days," he said. He might have been screaming or whispering, he couldn't tell. He could hardly hear his own voice. "It was eight days."

Then he left.

As he went out the front door, he felt someone touch his arm.

"Wunder. Wait." He turned to see Davy following him. He looked like he was about to burst into tears.

And Wunder never would have thought that he would make Davy cry, not Davy, who had been his best friend his whole life, who brought him newspaper cuttings of miracle stories, who would do anything for him. Never, ever, not in a million years.

But he did.

"Just leave me alone!" he yelled.

He ran to the bicycle rack, where, of course, Faye was waiting for him. She watched impassively as he unlocked his bike chain and yanked it off, as he jerked his bike free.

"Wundie," she said. "We need to talk."

Wunder didn't want to talk. He didn't want to keep asking himself question after question. He didn't want to keep trying *not* to ask himself question after question. He didn't want to wander around his house, the cemetery, his town like a ghost, angry and lonely and confused.

He was ready for some answers.

He shoved his hand into his pocket and pulled out the letter.

"Not now, Faye," Wunder said. "We need to deliver this."

Part Four

THE LETTERS

Chapter 21

"Florence isn't Sylvester," Faye said for the tenth time.

They were riding their bikes across town, away from the woods and cemetery, toward St. Gerard's.

"I know," Wunder said for the tenth time. "But they have the same last name, and I don't know any other Dabrowskis. Maybe they're related."

"So we're going to go to the church and ask for Florence Dabrowski?"

"Why not?" Wunder asked. "It's worth a try."

St. Gerard's was an old building, the oldest in town except for maybe the DoorWay House. It was, however, in considerably better shape. The outside was made of silver-flecked light stone that gleamed in the sun. A bell tower rose above the main building, its top a soft blue. The front door was blue too.

"Can we go in the sanctuary?" Faye asked as Wunder pulled the door open.

"In the church?" Wunder said. "We *can*, I guess. But I don't want to."

"I do," Faye said. "I've always wanted to see what it looks like in here."

She went in ahead of him, straight to the glass double doors that Wunder had not been through since his sister died. He followed her reluctantly, which seemed to be how he spent a lot of his time lately.

The inside of the church was even more beautiful than the outside. The stained-glass windows shone with rainbow light, dappling the wooden pews and white columns. Winks of gleaming gold added to the illumination, especially beyond the altar rails, in the sanctuary, where everything seemed to glow. There was a faint scent of incense, sweet and sharp and ever-present. And, like the door and the top of the bell tower, the vaulted ceiling, behind its wooden arches, was blue.

Wunder had always liked that about his church, that the highest places and the way in were the color of the sky. He sometimes imagined that all the words in the sanctuary—all the prayers and verses and songs—were carried up to the sky-blue ceiling, carried up and then out, out, streaming from the bell tower and flowing through the cracks in the front door, like wind, like smoke, rising up from the sky-blue paint into the sky-blue sky.

Where the sun shone. Where birds flew.

He wasn't surprised to see Faye pinning her bangs to one side and craning her neck this way and that, like she wanted to see every possible nook and cranny.

"It feels very supernatural in here, doesn't it?" she asked with a little shiver.

"I don't think so," Wunder said. He stayed at the back, and he didn't look up at the ceiling. "It just seems that way because of the decorations and the light."

"Wundie, you know that's not true."

Wunder didn't answer. And he still didn't look up.

Instead, he turned and went back through the glass doors.

Faye could stay for as long as she wanted. But he wasn't going to stay with her.

The church offices were not beautiful. They looked like normal offices, like the ones at Safe and Sound Insurance.

There was a woman sitting at a desk at the front. She was folding bulletins that read *All Souls' Day* and pictured white flowers and candles, but she stopped when they came in. Wunder knew her—Mrs. Ceiba. She had led his Sunday school class when he was in preschool. She used puppets in her lessons and gave out tiny cups of animal crackers.

"Wunder," she said. She gave him a sad smile. "I've been meaning to come by. How are you?"

"I'm fine," he said. He didn't want to talk about himself—not one bit—so he quickly continued, "We're here to see Florence Dabrowski. Do you know her?"

Mrs. Ceiba's expression went from sympathetic to distressed. "Florence?" she whispered. "You're looking for Florence? Well, I'm so sorry, but—did you know her? I'm so sorry."

"Why are you sorry?" Faye asked. "What happened?"

"Lydia, are you talking to me?"

A creaky bellow emitted from the door off to the side of Mrs. Ceiba's desk. Wunder recognized the voice. It was very recognizable. There was the sound of shuffling feet and a cane tapping, and then a shaggy, gray head leaned out the door.

It was the Minister of Consolation.

Chapter 22

"Oh my goodness! I'm so sorry we disturbed you!" Mrs. Ceiba had stood up. She was talking very loudly.

"I've told you, Lydia!" the minister yelled. "There's no need to yell. I can hear just fine!" His bespectacled eyes roamed around the room, stopping on Faye and Wunder. "Who are you?"

"This is Wunder Ellis," Mrs. Ceiba said, still very loudly. "And his friend—"

"Faye," Faye said.

"His friend Faye. Wunder, Faye, this is Mr. Dabrowski. He's in charge of our Ministry of Consolation."

"Dabrowski," Wunder repeated. "Do you know Florence?

Do you know Sylvester? We have something for him." He held up the letter.

The minister raised two bushy gray eyebrows at them. Mrs. Ceiba was wringing her hands together. She looked extremely uncomfortable.

"Come into my office!" he yelled. He shuffled back inside.

The office was a cramped room, entirely taken up by two threadbare armchairs, an old desk overflowing with papers, and a wooden chair. The minister stood at the door and glared as Wunder and Faye sat. Then he shut the door quite forcefully and began making his way back to his desk.

It took a while, and as he waited, Wunder stared across the paper-strewn desk. There was a picture of Saint Gerard on the wall. In the picture, the saint wore a long black robe and cradled a crucifix. Behind him, a woman and a peacefully slumbering infant lay on a bed. The woman was clutching a white handkerchief. The story of this picture, taken from the About Us section of the church bulletin, had featured in one of Wunder's earliest *Miraculous* entries:

Miraculous Entry #10

Saint Gerard performed many miracles. The most well-known involves a woman who met Saint Gerard

140

when she was a child. During this meeting, he gave her his handkerchief, telling her she might need it someday. Years later, after Saint Gerard had been dead for some time, the woman suffered complications during childbirth. Fearing for her life and for the life of her child, she remembered Saint Gerard's handkerchief. As soon as it was brought to her, her pain ceased, and she delivered a healthy baby.

Saint Gerard was the patron saint of pregnant women. He was the patron saint of childbirth.

"Let's have that letter!" The minister had finally made it to the wooden chair behind the desk. His hand was outstretched.

Wunder turned away from Saint Gerard.

"It's not for you," Faye said. "It's for Sylvester."

"I am Sylvester, you know," the minister replied. "And Florence was my wife. But she's dead."

Faye shrieked. Wunder shook his head.

"She can't be," he said. The minister didn't say anything. "She can't be!" he repeated, louder.

The minister glowered at him. "She can be. And she is."

Wunder knew that the minister was unlikely to be wrong about his own wife's mortality. But he unzipped his backpack and yanked out *The Miraculous*. He flipped it open to Entry #603 and thrust it across the desk.

"She was healed," he said.

There was silence in the little room as the minister took off his large black-rimmed glasses and put on small, gold-rimmed reading glasses. He studied the page. He studied it for a long time, much longer than was necessary to read such a short entry.

"What is this?" he asked finally.

"She was healed," Wunder insisted. It sounded like an accusation.

"It was a miracle," Faye added. And Wunder found himself nodding, as if he agreed with her.

The minister didn't answer. Maybe he didn't hear. He was still staring down at *The Miraculous*.

"You made this?" he asked.

Wunder nodded. "I'm—I used to be a miracologist." The minister glanced up, bushy eyebrows raised high in confusion. "I collected miracles."

The minister went back to the book, turning the pages one by one, stopping for a moment at each entry.

"She did get well, you know," he said. "For almost a year, she wasn't in pain. And she remembered more, remembered me. The doctors had never seen anything like it. I

142

never think about that really." He took off his glasses and looked up, from Wunder to Faye and then back. "I did your sister's funeral," he said, pointing at Wunder.

"Yes," Wunder said.

He pointed at Faye now. "What about you?"

"My grandfather died," Faye said. "But you didn't do any funerals for me. I don't go to church here. And even if I did, I wouldn't want you to anyway. You're extremely unconsoling."

As true as this was, Wunder thought it probably wasn't the best time to bring it up.

The minister, however, nodded. "You're right, you know!" he cried. "I was consoling once, I think. When Florence was alive. But now—" He held up his hands, empty, as if to show he had nothing.

"Why do you do it, then?" Faye asked.

"I started," the minister said, "when I retired. I wanted to do something useful, and the Church had need of me. It is a hard task, to console the grieving when the ones they love are gone. But I did my best. Then Florence passed. I don't do much consolation work these days. And I never go to the cemetery, unless I'm doing a funeral."

Wunder thought of the rows of graves, always deserted, always silent. "Why not?" he asked.

"She's not in the cemetery, you know," the minister said. "And I know that's as it should be; I know that she is somewhere far better. I do wish though"—he paused to glance behind him at the picture of the saint, a guilty look on his face—"I do wish there was a way she could be here too. I wish there was a way they could all be here."

For the first time in the conversation, Wunder felt like the minister might actually have something to offer him. He noticed that Faye had scooched to the front of her seat. Maybe this was what the witch wanted to talk to the minister about. Maybe Faye had been right. Dark, terrible things had happened—his sister had died, and Florence had died—but maybe the minister knew how to find miracles in that darkness.

"Do you ever feel," Wunder said slowly, tentatively, "like she could? Like she might be able to come back?"

Then he held his breath.

But the minister shook his head right away, his halo of gray hair bobbing his answer: no, no, no. "I don't," he said. "I feel like she is far away, very, very far away." He looked back down at *The Miraculous*, back at Entry #603. "I feel, sometimes, like everyone is very far away, you know. Like I am the only person on the earth."

144

Wunder let out his breath. Faye sat back in her seat. The room was silent.

Then Wunder did something he'd never done before. He pulled *The Miraculous* back to himself and very, very carefully ripped out Entry #603. "So you remember the miracle part," he said. "And here's your letter." He held both out to the minister.

The minister took them. He set the *Miraculous* page gently, reverently at the center of his desk. Then he opened the envelope with a silver letter opener.

The paper he took out had the same aged look as the envelope. When he unfolded it, the light shone through, and Wunder could see words scrawled in the same script as the name on the outside. He couldn't read them though.

The minister put his gold-rimmed glasses back on. Wunder watched as his eyes moved down the entire page, then went back to the top again. When he had completed his second reading, the minister yelled, "Who gave you this?"

"A woman from the DoorWay House," Wunder replied.

"The DoorWay House?" The minister took off his glasses and rubbed his eyes. "Have you read this letter?" he asked.

"No," Faye said. "It was sealed when we got it. But we're supposed to get one soon."

"And we know it's an invitation," Wunder said.

The minister nodded a few times. "Yes, but an invitation to what?" he said. He looked very old and very, very tired. "I suppose we shall see."

It was the quietest Wunder had ever heard him.

Chapter 23

The next day, Wunder didn't go past the cemetery. He didn't go into the woods. Delivering the letter hadn't given him the answers he'd hoped for. The Minister of Consolation—even with his knowledge and his position at the church—seemed to be as angry and confused as Wunder. The minister didn't have the answers.

But Wunder's questions hadn't gone away. In fact, they were louder than ever.

That was why he stayed away from the DoorWay House. He was afraid of how much he wanted to know what the witch was up to. He was afraid of how much he wanted to be wrong, how much he wanted the minister to be wrong.

He was afraid of how much he wanted to believe in miracles again.

Wunder wasn't sure what Faye was feeling, because she didn't try to talk to him at school or follow him after. She did give him a few slow waves of her black-gloved hand.

But the day after that, she was waiting at the bicycle racks.

"Let's go to the cemetery," she said.

"The cemetery?"

"Yes, Wundie. The cemetery. We need to talk about what to do next."

In the cemetery, Faye toe-dragged herself right up the hill, where she settled down next to the memorial stone. Wunder sat on the other side of her, as far from the stone as he could get. He didn't look at it or read the words, but they played over and over in his mind. *Behold, behold, behold* . . .

"I don't know if we should go back," he said. "To the DoorWay House, I mean."

"I knew you were going to say that, Wundie," Faye said. "And I didn't want to pressure you—I even gave you a whole day off—but we absolutely have to."

"I thought you were afraid of the witch," Wunder said. "I thought you said she wanted to poison us or steal our souls or whatever."

"I was afraid," Faye said. "Only because I know more about these kinds of things than you do. But now, more than ever, I think we have to see the witch."

Wunder sighed. "You're always saying that. We don't *have* to do anything."

"Yes, we do." Faye's voice grew more insistent. "We need to know what she's doing here. We need to know who she is. I know you say you don't believe in miracles anymore, but you went to see her. You delivered the letter."

Wunder shook his head. "I shouldn't have done that," he said. "But it doesn't matter. The minister—he said his wife is gone, gone for good. I don't know what the witch—I mean, the old woman—wanted with him, but it doesn't have any-thing to do with bringing people back from the dead, if you're still thinking that."

He turned even farther away from the stone. Now he was looking down over the woods, and from this angle he could see that the leaves had almost fully changed. Reds and golds had replaced green, the colors creating a botanical sunrise, a foliage wildfire. It was the woods at their most vibrant, their most beautiful. But soon, too soon, he knew, everything would be brown, everything would be dead, the trees would be bare.

"It doesn't," he repeated. Then, "Does it?"

"Maybe," Faye said. "Maybe not. But, Wundie, I think we both know that this is not the time to stop searching."

Wunder was quiet for a moment. Without his consent, his eyes wandered away from the dying forest and back to the stone. *We will all be changed* . . . He thought about what the witch had said: *There is much to discuss*. What did she want to tell him? What if he let himself listen? Could there truly be a miracle waiting to be found, bright and shining, after the darkness of his sister's death?

"Even after what the minister said, you still think the witch—the old woman—has something to do with my sister?" he asked. "And . . . resurrections?"

He looked over at Faye. Her hood was pulled up over her head and she was nodding.

"I do, Wundie," she said. "I do."

And Wunder found himself nodding along. Because, he realized, he did too. "We'll go back, then," he said.

Chapter 24

They met in the woods on Saturday morning. It was the coldest day that autumn yet, too cold for October. Wunder shivered in his sky-blue jacket; he hadn't anticipated such low temperatures. Faye seemed toasty in a poufy purple coat covered in sparkly turquoise hearts and her black cloak.

When Wunder arrived, she handed him something small and shiny. It was a flat silver hand. The spread fingers were covered in intricate designs, and a bright blue stone eye punctuated the palm.

"I brought these," Faye said. She held up one of her own.

"What are they?" Wunder asked, lifting the eye to his own eye.

"Hamsa amulets, otherwise known as Hands of Fatima or Hands of Miriam. They'll protect us from spells and the evil eye and other witchcraft."

Wunder lowered his amulet and frowned. "She's not a witch, remember?"

"I remember that *you* think she's not a witch," Faye said. "You should remember that I still think she might be one, although there are, as we have discussed, other possibilities. When this saves you from all kinds of hexes and jinxes and curses, you'll thank me."

The witch was on her porch, as always. She smiled when she saw them. She had, Wunder noticed, perfect teeth, small and white and even.

"You are back," she said in her faraway voice. "I am glad. Yes, yes, yes. I am glad. Come in."

When they walked through the house's door, Wunder felt the stone of his heart begin to rattle the same way it had on the first visit. This time, he wrapped both arms around himself. He was there for answers. He didn't want to get sidetracked by his heart.

The house looked exactly the same. It didn't seem like the witch was doing much settling in. There was no new furniture, and the dust was still thick and heavy, blanketing everything like a winter snow, burying everything like earth on a grave. Wunder could see his own footprints from five days ago in it.

"I saw you two pass my trail the other day," the witch said as they entered the little kitchen. She gestured for them to sit at the table, which was still covered in newspapers. "Leaving the cemetery, I think."

"We've been spending a lot of time among the dead," Faye told her. "The first time we were both there was for Wundie's sister's funeral." She paused and stared at the witch, hard. The witch stared back until Faye continued, "I was there because of my grandfather. But I think you know that."

"I know," the witch said. She turned on the water at the sink to fill the teakettle. "Yes, yes, yes. Almost everyone I see is going to a funeral. That is the sadness of living by a cemetery. The sadness and the beauty."

This didn't make sense to Wunder. *Sadness* and *beauty* did not go together. "What's so beautiful about a cemetery?" he asked.

"It is where the dead are remembered by those who love them," the witch said. She lit the rust-coated stove and placed the kettle on the flames. "It is where the living connect to the ones they love. This is beautiful, I think."

Wunder shook his head. "The Minister of Consolation—I

mean, Sylvester Dabrowski, the one you sent the letter to—
he thinks that when people die, they're gone. He said he
doesn't even go to the cemetery, because he knows his
wife's not there. She's in a better place."

"That is one way to think of it," the witch said. "Did that
seem to bring him some comfort?"

"No," Wunder admitted. "He was very sad. And angry."

"It is not an easy thing to believe the dead have gone
far, far away, even if it is to a better place. No, no, no. We
want them here, with us." She came to sit across from
them. Her wrinkled hands rested on the obituaries spread
out before her. "But there are many ways to think about
death."

"I think death is terrible," Faye said. One hand was tucked
in her cloak, and Wunder knew she was holding on to her
amulet.

"For the living, it often is," the witch said. "But the dead
may feel differently."

Here was another thing Wunder had never thought of
before. He had never imagined that the tiny, helpless baby
he had spent hours watching in the hospital could have any
feelings about her own death.

"You mean because they're in heaven?" he asked.

The witch shrugged, her thin shoulders rising and falling

under her white robe and shawls. "Heaven, maybe," she said. "I have not been that far; I do not know exactly. But"— she leaned across the table toward them, and her dark eyes were bright—"how do you know that is all there is? How do you know it is death and then—zip—straight to heaven? Maybe there are other branches to climb up, other roots to follow down. Other places, other lives, other ways of being."

"Like zombies?" Faye asked, her voice shrill. "Like ghosts? Like *resurrections*? What? What else happens?"

The witch shrugged again. "Zombies, I don't know," she said. "Ghosts, resurrections, maybe, maybe. But there is far more than heaven and earth, I think. Yes, yes, yes. Far, far more."

Wunder knew that this was the time to demand answers. This was the time to ask the witch about the memorial stone, to ask her who she was. But in that spiraling house, with his heart shaking and the witch's black eyes staring into his, he couldn't seem to find the words.

And when Faye spoke, her voice was quiet again, slow and dreamy. "My grandfather used to do these ceremonies for the dead," she said. "He would set out special foods for his parents on the anniversaries of their deaths and on holidays. *Jesa*, that's what it's called. I helped him sometimes, but my mother never did." She pulled her cloak tighter around herself. "My grandfather believed in a lot of things."

The witch nodded slowly through this pause-filled discourse. The teakettle began to whistle, and she rose gracefully to her feet. "There are many ways to think about death," she repeated as she took the kettle from the stove. "I prefer the ways that remember the dead, like your grandfather's, like so many beautiful celebrations and rituals and rites from around the world and throughout history. I prefer the ways that do not forget the great powers of memory and love."

While the witch prepared the tea, Wunder tried to focus on what he wanted to ask her, but instead he found himself thinking about his sister again, his sister and memory and love. He remembered her—of course he did. He thought about her every day. And he had loved her. He had loved her more in her eight days of life than he would have thought possible.

But he had not wanted to go to her funeral. He had not wanted to do the celebrations and rituals and rites. He had not wanted anyone to do them. He had not thought they would help.

Because in the end, death was still death. Wasn't it?

"It is good that you should come here to share these things with me," the witch said, bringing Wunder out of his thoughts. She set two steaming cups in front of them. "Because it has everything to do with what I want to share with you. There is something that I need, something to do with the DoorWay Tree. Let us have some tea, and I will tell you about it. Yes, yes, yes. I feel that you two may be the ones who can help me."

"What is it?" Wunder asked. He reached for his cup, eager to hear what the witch would say next.

"Stop!"

Faye had shrieked this word. Her hands were out of her pockets and she was gripping her amulet in plain sight.

"Faye—" Wunder started.

"No!" Faye used her other hand to pry his fingers from his teacup and moved it to the other side of her. "No tea! No weird, witchy favors!"

The witch seemed startled, but she held her hands up. "I understand," she said. "You are not ready. I can wait. Not for long, but I can wait. But tell me"—she smiled, her perfect teeth shining white in her wrinkled face—"what makes you think I am a witch?"

"I don't think you're a witch," Wunder said quickly.

Faye frowned at him and then at the witch. "Really?" she

asked her. "Have you seen yourself? Have you seen this place?"

"I don't know much about witches," the witch admitted. "But I suppose I can see why you might think such a thing." She sat back down across from them, still smiling. "The invitations though. Perhaps you will not do any new favors for me, but I have more letters. Many more . . ." She trailed off, a question in her silence.

"We can deliver more letters," Wunder said. "If that's what you want."

"That is what I want," she said. She reached into her layers of clothing and pulled out another envelope. "That would help me very much."

Wunder took the letter and tucked it into his pocket. Maybe he wasn't ready to demand answers from the witch, but her words had given him something already. His mind was buzzing with these new ideas, new possibilities, new questions. And he could do this. He could deliver her letters. He could keep searching through the dark this way.

"Come back after you deliver this one," she said. "If your hesitations are gone, if you are ready, I have more. I have many, many more. Yes, Faye?"

Faye pushed the teacups a little farther down the table.

Then she put her hand and the hand-shaped amulet back in her pocket. "I suppose," she said, "that we can do that."

When they left the witch's house, there was a flurry of movement, the same as last time. Except it wasn't on the path ahead but in the bushes on the dirt trail. Davy ran his bike past the live oak, then pedaled off without looking behind him.

"Is he spying on us?" Faye asked. "What's wrong with him?"

"I think he misses me," Wunder said, watching as his friend disappeared from sight. "Davy is—well, he *was* one of my best friends."

"He doesn't seem as bad as the other one—what's his name?" She flipped her hair, but in slow motion.

"Tomás," Wunder said.

Faye nodded. "That's the one," she said. "Davy doesn't seem as bad as him. Maybe you should let him deliver letters with us. Isn't he a paperboy? I bet he knows where everyone lives."

Wunder didn't answer. Davy seemed like part of another life, the best friend of another boy. A boy whose father had been home in time for dinner every night. A boy whose mother always had a smile and a hug and a new book to share. A life where everything was connected and bright. He wasn't sure where Davy would fit into his new life, where everything seemed separate and strange.

He hardly knew how he fit into it himself.

That night, he took out the envelope. It was the same as the first—cream-colored, timeworn, sealed with the spread-out tree.

And scrawled in that same black handwriting was a name that made him shake his head in disbelief.

He knew exactly where to deliver this letter.

Then he got out *The Miraculous*. He flipped through it until he found what he was looking for.

When he was ready to sleep, he set them both—the letter and the book—on his nightstand.

Chapter 25

He found Faye on Monday before school started. "You're not going to like our next letter delivery," he said.

"Because the first one was so fun?"

"This one will be worse . . . for you, at least," Wunder said.

"Who is it?" Faye asked.

"Eugenia Simone," Wunder said. "Also known as Eugenia the Pink Priss."

Faye pulled her cloak hood over her face. "You've got to be kidding me," she said from inside the velvet and satin.

* * *

When they entered the town hall that afternoon, Eugenia was at her desk. This time, she didn't even pretend to give them a bright pink smile. She glared immediately.

"I cannot believe you two criminals have the audacity to return to the scene of the crime," she said, rising to her feet and picking up her phone. "I am calling security right this instant. Didn't your crystal ball tell you that?"

"I would love to have a crystal ball," Faye said, "but my mother doesn't approve of things related to the occult."

"Like her daughter?" Eugenia began to dial.

"We have something for you!" Wunder said quickly. "That's why we're here! To deliver this invitation."

Eugenia's pink-nailed finger paused. "From whom?"

"From the witch of the DoorWay House," Faye said. Her expression revealed nothing, but Wunder could tell she was enjoying herself.

"Don't test me, young lady," Eugenia snapped. "I know you two broke in here. I know you stole government property. And I *had* dropped the matter, but I will not hesitate—"

"I'm sorry about your father," Wunder interrupted her.

Eugenia's bright pink mouth dropped open. Her eyes went wide. "What about him?" she said.

"I know that he—that he died," Wunder said. "I also

know that he escaped a fire once. Miraculously—well, according to him."

Eugenia stared at him, uncertain, wary. "How do you know that?"

Wunder set his backpack on the ground. He unzipped it and pulled out *The Miraculous*. Then he flipped it open to one of the pages he had marked the night before. It was a newspaper clipping.

"I get the paper every week," he said. "And I've also searched through the back issues—well, just the Community News section, actually. I was—I am—I was a miracologist."

He set *The Miraculous* on Eugenia's desk. She kept her eyes on him for a moment more, then pulled the book toward herself and began to read silently:

Miraculous Entry #272

The owner of Simone's Stationery, Quincy Simone, experienced what he calls "a miracle" on Wednesday night. The lifetime Branch Hill resident says that when he went to bed in the over-store apartment, he set his alarm for 6:00 a.m., as he does every evening.

However, the store owner reports that his alarm went off around 3:20 a.m. Unaware of the time, Simone got

163

ready for work and was heading to the store downstairs when he smelled smoke. He immediately called 911.

Firefighters responded quickly and were able to confine a small electrical fire to a back storeroom. Simone, his wife, and their three children were unharmed. The family home and the majority of the store were undamaged.

Wunder could tell when Eugenia was done reading only because her eyes stopped moving back and forth. She didn't look up from *The Miraculous*.

"And I know that you also got a scholarship to college," he said. His mouth was dry. He had no idea if this was what he was supposed to be doing. He only knew that he had told the witch he would deliver the letter. "There was an article about that too." He turned to the other page he'd marked, leaving the book in front of her. "You said it was a miracle. Although I think it was probably just because you worked hard."

Miraculous Entry #465

Congratulations are in order for Eugenia Simone, daughter of Quincy and Rita Simone. The eighteen-year-old Oak Wood High School graduate was

164

recently accepted to Fraxinus College with a full
scholarship.

"I'm so happy," the elated teen told this reporter. "It's
an absolute miracle!"

Well done, Eugenia! The town of Branch Hill wishes
you all the best.

"I thought it was a miracle," Eugenia said, running her
finger along the edge of the newspaper clipping, "because
I was never very good in school. I didn't think I'd even get
into college, let alone get a scholarship. I wasn't even
going to apply."

"Two miracles, then," Wunder said.

Eugenia looked up now, and her eyes were wet and
gleaming. "He died while I was in college," she said. "My
senior year." She grimace-smiled again, but it didn't seem
mean like it had when Wunder first met her. It seemed like
she didn't know what to do next. "Doesn't seem fair, does
it?" she continued. "That those wonderful things could happen to him, to me. And then that awful, terrible thing, and
now he's gone, gone forever. What am I supposed to do
with that?"

Wunder shook his head. "I don't know," he said. "I don't
know either. But I have this." He held the letter out.

"Thank you," she said, taking it.

"And do you have a pair of scissors?"

He cut out both entries for her. Then she watched them walk away, papers pressed to her heart. She didn't call security. She didn't say another word.

"Have you noticed anything about these letters?" Wunder asked Faye as they climbed onto their bikes. "I mean, about the people we're delivering them to?"

"No," Faye said. She was much more subdued than Wunder had expected her to be after a meeting with Eugenia the Pink Priss.

"They're all to people who have lost someone," Wunder said. "And they've all experienced a miracle."

"We've only delivered two letters so far though," Faye replied. "I don't know if you can draw conclusions from a sample size of two."

"Rationality does not suit you, Faye," Wunder said. He smiled, just a small smile. Then he pushed off on his bike. The wind was cool and gusty and lifting.

"But what does the letter say?" Faye asked, catching up to him. "Why don't we read it?"

"I don't know," Wunder said. "Why haven't we?"

"I thought it might curse us," Faye said. "Like a magic-booby-trap kind of thing."

"Do you still think that?"

166

"I'm not sure," Faye said.

"They're not addressed to us," Wunder pointed out. "And we're going to get our own eventually."

"Well, let's say you're right," Faye said. "Let's say that the witch is handing out letters to the family members of the miraculous dead." She paused a moment. The wind whistled past Wunder's ears. "How would she know about all that? She just got here. How does she know all about this town? Have you thought"—she paused again—"have you thought any more about who she is, Wundie? I mean, who she *really* is?"

Wunder had. He had thought about it a lot.

But if the witch was who Faye was hinting she was, if the witch was who Wunder sometimes almost let himself think she could be, then that would be the biggest miracle of all. And after so much anger and sadness, Wunder knew he wasn't ready to think about that.

Because if he believed that his sister had come back to life and then it wasn't true, he didn't think he would ever, ever recover.

And yet, here he was, delivering letters. Here he was, looking forward to returning to the DoorWay House to tell the witch that he'd done it, to ask her what she wanted him to do next.

"I know what you think," he said. "But we don't know anything yet."

Faye rolled her smudge-rimmed eyes. "Wundie. Come on. We know a lot of things. We know that the witch showed up the day of your sister's funeral. We know the witch wants you to hand out these crazy miracle-survivor letters. We know she lives in a magic house covered in spinny, spirally circles. Et cetera. That's a lot of things we know."

"But it's not enough," Wunder replied. "Those things could be coincidences."

"What about the memorial stone?" Faye said. "You've never asked why she did that, why she used your sister's name."

"You're right," Wunder said. "We should at least ask about that. We will ask about that. Soon."

Chapter 26

They went to the DoorWay House the very next day. The witch was on her porch. She didn't ask them to come inside. She didn't ask them to have tea with her. Instead, she held out a stack of letters.

"I think you are ready for these now," she said. "Am I right?"

Wunder glanced over at Faye. She nodded. "Are ours in here?" he asked.

The witch raised her eyebrows and studied them with her black eyes.

"Not yet," she said finally. "Soon, I think. Yes, soon, soon, soon. But deliver these first, then come back for more. I have many, many more. And I am running out of time."

Wunder and Faye took the letters and *The Miraculous* and set off. They didn't have to discuss where they were headed. They both knew that the cemetery was the only place to do this work.

"There may be quicker ways to find these names," Wunder said, opening *The Miraculous* on the bristly brown grass at the top of the hill, next to the memorial stone. "But if they're in here, then I want to know about it."

And they were. As the afternoon wore on, Faye and Wunder found that every name on every letter had a corresponding entry. Every person was connected, somehow, to a miracle. And, Wunder was sure, every person had also lost someone, someone they loved.

Wunder cut the entries out of *The Miraculous*, and Faye stapled them to the envelopes. Then they delivered the letters, the entire stack, that day.

And the next day, they went back to the DoorWay House for more.

Every day that week, the witch gave them letters. Letter after letter after letter. Letters to teachers and letters to neighbors. A letter to the owner of the Snack Shack and a letter to Wunder's mother's boss, Mrs. Atkins. A letter to Ms. Shunem and a letter to Vice Principal Jefferson. Letters to workers at SunShiners and letters to doctors at the hospital. A letter to Father Robles, who hugged Wunder and didn't say a word about the Sundays he'd missed, and a letter to Faye's pastor, Pastor Chung, who accepted it with a look of weary resignation at Faye's cloak.

Often, Wunder wouldn't recognize the name on a letter. But then he would open *The Miraculous*. He would turn page after page after silver-leafed page until he found the miracle connected to the name. He would read the story and remember the first time he'd heard it.

Most letters, he and Faye would leave without a word. Wunder would tape the envelopes to the doors, because he didn't want them to blow away.

But sometimes, the recipients were there.

"I don't know what this says," Wunder would say, "but I know you've seen miracles and I know you've seen loss. And I think this letter has to do with both."

He would stay sometimes while they read *The Miraculous* entry, while they read the letter. And he would feel the ghost of that old feeling, the feeling that he was connecting the dots of people's souls.

It was different though. Before, he had collected the miracles for himself. Now he was sharing them.

One afternoon, he and Faye were in the cemetery, searching through *The Miraculous* for the most recent batch of names.

"I wonder if my mom will get a letter," Faye said. She was

lying on her stomach in the stubbly grass next to the stone, her cloak streaming behind her like a parachute.

"*Your* mom?" Wunder asked. He had in fact been thinking of his own mother ever since he realized who was getting the letters. He had been thinking about delivering a letter to her, an envelope with *Austra Ellis* written on it, the black tree reaching out.

"Yes, *my* mom," Faye said. "Her father died, remember? My grandfather?"

"I know," Wunder said, although he hadn't remembered in that moment. He tried to make it up to her by asking, "But you were closer to him than she was, right?"

Faye was quiet for a long time, even longer than she was usually quiet. "I was close to him in one way," she replied, "and she was close to him in another. But we don't really get along, my mom and me. My grandfather never liked that. That was something he said to me before he died. He said, 'This will bring you closer together. That's what losing someone does.'" She wrapped her cloak around herself, tight, tight. "But I don't think it has."

"Maybe you're close to her the same way she was close to him," Wunder suggested.

"Hold on, Wundie. Let me think about that for a minute," Faye said. Then she sighed. "No, I don't think we are. She thinks I'm a weirdo. What about you and your parents? Are you close?"

"We were," Wunder said. He thought about how his father had been trying to be around more but still worked late most nights. He thought about how his mother had come out of her room a few times to watch television or eat with him, but how she didn't talk much or smile and how she always went back to her room, how she always shut the door again.

"You still are," Faye assured him. "I'm sure you still are." He hoped she wouldn't say that Milagros's death would connect them. And she didn't. Not exactly. What she said was "Maybe we haven't gotten to the close part yet. Maybe it takes a while."

"Maybe," Wunder said doubtfully. "But the people we've delivered letters to, so many of them seem sad and lonely. And we never see them here, in the cemetery. Everyone stays away. It doesn't seem like losing someone brings people together. It seems like it pushes them apart."

When Faye didn't answer right away, Wunder looked over to find that her hood was up. She was completely hidden, a wind-blown, black cocoon.

"My mom never talks about my grandfather," she said, barely audible. "She didn't even want to come to the graveyard on his birthday. How can his death bring us closer if she's afraid to think about him?" The next thing she said was so soft, so near-silent that Wunder had to put his head down next to hers to hear it. "I think about him a lot."

Wunder didn't sit back up. He stretched out on the ground, his hands fiddling with the blades of dry grass, his eyes on the black velvet of the hood. "I think about Milagros too," he said. "Even though at first, I didn't want to come to the cemetery either. And now I am, but my dad hasn't been back and my mom has never come. And they don't talk about her. They don't talk about anything."

There was no answer from the cocoon.

Wunder worried suddenly that he had offended her. He thought of what Tomás had said, that he'd known Milagros for only eight days. Faye had known her grandfather for her whole life. What if she thought he couldn't possibly understand how she felt?

"I know—I know it's different," he said, fumbling for words, "losing a baby sister and losing a grandfather. But I think some of what we feel is the same."

Faye pulled her hood off and got to her knees. Her face was flushed and her eyes were bright and wet. "Of course it is, Wundie," she said. "That's why we're doing this together.

Eight days or eight hundred years doesn't matter." She reached into her cloak and pulled out a bobby pin.

When her hair was back, she stared down at him, right into his eyes, and asked, "What does time have to do with love?"

And Wunder found himself smiling the tiniest smile back up at her. He didn't need to worry about offending Faye. They had both been beckoned to the DoorWay House. They were both waiting for their letters. They had become friends in a cemetery. Faye understood. Even if she did call him Wundie.

"Nothing," he said.

"Nothing, Wundie," Faye agreed. Then she took the next letter out of a cloak pocket. "Now let's get back to work."

Chapter 27

The Miraculous *was back on* Wunder's *nightstand* all the time now. He found himself reading through it even when he wasn't searching for letter recipients. He never went to the last entry—he couldn't do that yet; he didn't want to do that ever. But he read everything that came before.

He told himself he still didn't believe in the miracles, but his heart seemed to think otherwise. While he read, the stone of his heart would grow warmer; the stone of his heart would stir and shift.

And he was getting braver, delivering letters and sharing entries. He was getting closer and closer to being ready,

ready to ask the witch for the truth, the whole truth, about who she was and what she wanted.

After dinner one night, Wunder was flipping through a new stack of letters. He separated them into names he recognized—Alex Lin, Susan Holt, Mateo Ramos—and names he didn't—Margot Arvid, Charlie Darrow, Afnan Khan. He knew the names he recognized must have entries in *The Miraculous*, but he couldn't think of any of them off the top of his head.

Until he came to the last letter in the pile:

Mariah Lazar

He knew Mariah Lazar. She wasn't in *The Miraculous* exactly, but her children were.

She had twins. Wunder had interviewed them at school last year. They had been in first grade, and he had been in fifth. Their teacher, Mr. Raavi, had once been Wunder's teacher. He had listened to Wunder talk about his mira-cology, and he had seen *The Miraculous* once when Wunder brought it in for show-and-tell. After that, he had often brought Wunder stories to add to his book. The Lazar twins' story had been one of them.

Wunder found it in *The Miraculous*. It went like this:

Wunder: I am here with Jayla and Jayden Lazar to hear their account of their miraculous birth.

giggling from Jayla and Jayden

Wunder: Jayla, Jayden, can you tell me how old you are?

Jayla and Jayden (together): Seven.

Wunder: And where were you two born?

Jayden and Jayla (together): Branch Hill Hospital.

Wunder: Would you please describe the circumstances of your unusual birth?

Jayden: We only know what our mom told us—

Jayla: Because we were babies! We don't remember.

Wunder: I understand. Please tell me what your mother has told you.

Jayla: Well, we were born early—

Jayden: Really early. Only twenty-six weeks. It's supposed to be forty weeks—

Jayla: Twins come early most of the time, but not that early. And we were really, really tiny, not even two pounds. We were the smallest babies ever born at Branch Hill Hospital. We weren't breathing when we came out and they had to hook us up to machines—

Jayden: Like robots! And we were in the hospital for a long time, like months and months. But Jayla was in longer . . . something happened to her.

Jayla: Something in my heart, my mom says. So I had to stay, but Jayden got to go home.

Jayden: But then she came home too. You came home, Jayla.

Jayla: I did. I came home too. We both did.

At the time, it had just been one more miracle. There were always miracles about babies—babies born to mothers who thought they would never have babies, like his own mother; babies who survived horrible catastrophes unharmed; babies who lived when doctors predicted they would die. If you only read about miracles, you would think that babies always defied the odds.

Wunder knew now that they didn't. But Jayden and Jayla had.

So why was their mother getting a letter?

Wunder left his room and went to the kitchen. The visitors had stopped after a few days, the casseroles after two weeks, but the cards kept coming in, even now. There was a huge pile of them on the kitchen table. He sifted through until he found what he was looking for.

It was the card that had come with the casserole on the day of the funeral. It read:

No one can ever know exactly what another person is going through, but I do know about loss. When you are ready, please reach out to me. I would love to connect.

It was signed *Mariah Lazar.* Her phone number and address were there.

Wunder decided to go right away.

Chapter 28

The Lazar house was across town. Wunder rode his bike. He pedaled fast and with every rotation of the wheels, a new question came to him. It seemed to him that this was the letter he had been waiting for, the one that would hold answers. Here was a mother whose children had been saved. Here was a mother who had written to his own mother. Here, he hoped, was the end of his search.

When Jayla opened the door, he felt like a primed pump. He felt like an overwhelmed dam.

"Hi, Wunder!" Jayla cried. "Are you here to interview me and Jayden again?"

"No, Jayla," Wunder said. "Not this time. I need to talk to your mom."

Mariah Lazar was younger than Wunder had expected her to be, tall with long dark braids. She smiled when she saw him, the small, sad smile that Wunder was used to seeing now. She leaned on the door frame.

"Wunder Ellis," she said. "It's so good to finally meet you."

"You brought us a casserole," Wunder said.

She nodded. "I did. Sorry about that; I'm a dreadful cook. I also lead a grief group at the community center, although there aren't many people in it."

Wunder thought of the letters he had delivered, the dozens of people around town who had lost someone. "Why aren't there?" he asked, surprised.

"It's easy to connect over the things that make us happy. It's much harder to reach out when we're sad. Even though that's what we need." She held her hands open. It looked to Wunder as if she was inviting him to hug her and also showing that she wasn't hiding anything up her sleeves. "I'm hoping your parents will come and join us. When they're ready, of course."

"My dad has been working all the time," Wunder found himself saying. "And I don't know if my mother will ever be ready."

"People handle grief in different ways," Mariah replied. "Some want to be surrounded by friends and family. Some want to keep busy. Some want to be alone. Which is fine—for a while."

Wunder thought about telling her how his father seemed so lost and so lonely when he was at home. He thought about telling her how his mother still spent most of her time in her room, about how she would try to ask him about his day, then end up crying. But then he remembered why he was really there. He remembered that he was looking for answers.

"Jayla and Jayden were miracles," he said. "But you run a grief group. And I have a letter here for you. So I know that something else must have happened to you, something very unmiraculous."

Mariah took the letter. She let out a small sigh. "It was before the twins," she told him. "I lost a daughter, like your mother lost your sister."

Wunder knew who it was. It came to him right in that moment. He could picture the gravestone: no dates, the flying bird.

"Avery," he said.

Now it was Mariah who looked surprised, but she didn't ask him how he knew. "Avery."

Then he couldn't hold back anymore. "But do you think she's gone?" he said. His voice sounded strange, not the flat, crushed voice of the last few weeks, but jagged and sharp, a broken voice. "Forever? Have you ever felt like she could come back? Or do you just feel sad? Do you just feel angry? Do you just feel lonely and confused all the time?"

He was out of breath. He stared up at Mariah Lazar, gasping in the cool air, and she looked down at him, no longer smiling, but not upset either.

"Those are a lot of questions," she said. "And I would have to say that the answer to all of them is yes."

"How can it be yes?" Wunder asked. "How can it all be yes?"

Mariah straightened up from the doorway. She leaned toward Wunder. "I have to believe," she said, "that there are things I don't fully understand about life and death. When I lost Avery, yes, it felt like she was gone. Gone for good, gone forever. And then some days"—she bent her neck so that she was even closer to him—"some days I will hear a bird sing or feel a raindrop and it will seem, for a moment, like she's here. But it's so quick. It's not much." She opened her hands again. "But some things help. Jayden and Jayla help. And that's why I started the grief group."

"That's how you remember the dead," Wunder said.

"That's how I remember Avery," she agreed. "There are so many beautiful and true ways to feel close to our lost loved ones."

Wunder felt tired. He felt too tired to ask more questions. He liked what Mariah Lazar had said. But it wasn't enough. None of it was enough. "Thank you for talking to me," he said.

"You're welcome, Wunder," she said. "Anytime."

She waited until he was on his bike before she shut the door. She shut it very gently. He didn't even hear it click closed.

And Wunder knew as he pedaled home that the answers he was looking for weren't going to come from the families of the miraculous dead. He knew that he had spent enough time trying not to believe and he had spent enough time trying to find answers on his own. The only thing that would be enough was to talk to the witch—to ask her why she was there and what she wanted from him and who she was. To ask if she was his sister.

But still, still, still he didn't know if he could.

Because if none of it was enough, then she was his last hope. She was his very last hope.

Chapter 29

Halloween was on a Wednesday that year, and Golden Fig Middle School had a costume party on the Friday before. Wunder wasn't planning on going, but Faye had insisted.

"Listen, Wundie. We have to go," she'd said. "I have the best costume, but you're the only one who will get it. So if you're not there, no one will get it. Which I'm used to, but it would be nice to have someone get it. For once in my life."

"Okay, okay. I'll go. I'll get it," Wunder had said. "But I'm not wearing a costume this year."

"Mine will be supernaturally spectacular enough for both of us," Faye had assured him.

And when she walked into the school gym that Friday night, Wunder had to admit, her costume was pretty supernaturally spectacular. And he had to agree: No one else would get it.

Faye wore a white dress. Around her arms, torso, and waist, she had wrapped white cloth napkins, a white bandanna, and even white toilet paper. She had a wig of long black hair, and her face was covered in painted-on lines— lines from her nose to her mouth, lines around her eyes, lines across her forehead. Wrinkle lines. She was carrying a stack of envelopes in her hand.

Wunder laughed. "Everyone probably thinks you're a mummy," he said.

"With this hair?" Faye tossed her inky-black locks back. "Not a chance."

"What's in the envelopes?" he asked.

She opened one. It was empty.

"I couldn't think what to write, even to pretend," she said.

They walked around the gym, getting candy from the plastic cauldrons set up here and there. Everyone was in costume except for Wunder, but even in masks and face paint and wigs, he recognized each kid there. By now, he had delivered letters to dozens of their family members: to Charlotte Atkins's mother and to Ivo Reis's grandfather and to Mason Nash's uncle. And if he kept delivering letters, Wunder realized that eventually, at some point in their lives, every single one of his classmates would get their own. Each person in this room would experience a miracle, maybe many miracles. And each, he knew, would experience a terrible, terrible loss.

"Oh, hey, Wunder."

Wunder turned from faces he recognized to one of the faces he knew best of all. Davy was wearing a trash bag filled with crumpled-up paper. It was, Wunder realized, the same costume he'd worn last year.

Davy was rock.

Last year, Wunder had been paper. Tomás had been scissors.

"I know it was probably dumb to wear this costume," Davy said. "No one knows what I am without scissors and paper. But I couldn't think of anything else. You usually plan our costumes."

Suddenly, Wunder felt guilt, hard and knotted, in the pit of his stomach. Davy was his friend. Davy had been his friend for his whole life. And he had yelled at him and ignored him, and now here he was wearing a costume meant for three all by himself.

"It's not dumb," Wunder told him.

"You look like a bag of trash," Faye said. "Is that what you're supposed to be, David? A bag of trash?"

"No," Davy said. He sounded miserable. "Rock. I'm a rock."

"You haven't been very nice to Wundie," Faye said, holding up a white-gloved finger. "He's had some hard times. Some extremely hard times. And what did his friends do? They turned their backs on him, abandoned him, left him no choice but to become friends with me, et cetera."

"I don't know if that's how it happened," Wunder said.

But Davy was gnawing on his lip and gripping the sides of his trash bag. "It's true!" he cried. "I've been a terrible friend. I know it and you know it! When my mom was sick, you always talked to me about her, Wunder. But I was—you know I get nervous. I didn't know what to say. I'm sorry."

"That's okay, Davy," Wunder said. "I guess I didn't know what to say either." It felt, as he said this, like the gym grew a little brighter. He glanced around. "Where's Tomás? I haven't seen him."

Davy shrugged. "Tomás doesn't hang out with me anymore. Did you know he made the soccer team? He's got a lot of new friends."

Wunder felt the knot of guilt return. Davy had lost both of his best friends at once. "I'm really sorry, Davy," he said.

Davy shrugged again. "I kind of saw that one coming," he said.

"Me too," Wunder said.

They headed over to the refreshment table. Vice Principal Jefferson was there, serving punch with floating eyeballs. He was dressed as a vampire, including a long red cape.

"Nice mummy costume, Miss Lee!" he called to Faye.

"Nice cape-not-cloak, Mr. Jefferson," Faye said. "But I'm not a mummy. I'm a witch."

Davy gripped a skeleton-print paper plate and gawked at Faye as if he were seeing her for the first time. "A witch? Are you the DoorWay House witch?"

Faye smiled smugly at Wunder. "See? Everyone thinks she's a witch."

"What have you two been doing over there?" Davy's voice was shaky. "That place always gave me the heebie-jeebies, even before she showed up. And then she started asking about Wunder—"

"Asking about me?" Wunder said, confused.

"I've been trying to tell you—I deliver her paper. She's always out on her porch. I keep trying to go earlier and earlier so I don't have to see her. Today I went at 5:00 a.m., but she was already out there! I mean, it was dark and everything!"

190

"Get to the point, David," Faye said.

"She—she asked about Wunder," Davy said. "The day the obituary—after your sister was in the paper, Wunder. She asked me if I was your friend, and she asked if you believed in miracles. And then she had me bring an envelope to the town hall. I don't know what it was."

"For the memorial stone!" Faye shrieked.

Wunder was trying to understand what Davy was telling him, but ghosts and angels and demons and goblins were running all around him and the gym was so loud and suddenly darker again.

"You deliver the paper there?" he asked. "Since when?"

"Maybe a month," Davy said.

"When exactly?" Faye demanded.

Davy looked uncomfortable. "The day after—after Wunder's sister—after she . . . died."

"She showed up *the day after* Wundie's sister died?" Faye shouted.

"I—I guess so," Davy said, bewildered. "That's the first day I delivered her paper, anyway. And since then, she's had me deliver a million letters. And look"—he pulled an envelope out of the pocket of his gray sweatpants—"when I brought her the paper this morning, she gave me this one. It's for my mother."

It was a cream-colored envelope with a black wax seal. And scrawled across the front: *Tabitha Baum.*

For weeks, Wunder and Faye had delivered letters that they had not opened. They had waited for their own. For his part, Wunder had been afraid to know what was inside, afraid to solve the mystery, and it seemed like Faye must have felt that way too, because she hadn't pushed him.

But this new information from Davy seemed to be her tipping point.

"Open it!" she screamed.

Davy was so startled that he fell backward into the punch-and-snack table. His paper-filled trash bag suit crinkled and crunched. Faye snatched the envelope.

"That's my mother's!" Davy protested, knocking over a bowl of chips in his effort to right himself. But Faye was already ripping it open.

Inside was a piece of the same worn paper folded into thirds that everyone else had received. Wunder and Davy gathered around Faye as she unfolded it. There, in the same sprawling black handwriting, were the words:

"Behold! I tell you a miracle. We will not all sleep, but we will all be changed."

And under it:

Come to the highest point of Branch Hill Cemetery at

sunrise on the second of November. In this place of remem-
brance and love, we will experience miracles, and we will all
be changed. Together.

"The cemetery?" Davy asked. "What does it have to do
with my mom?"

Wunder shook his head, eyes on the letter. "I don't know,"
he said. "I guess because she's a miracle."

"A miracle? You mean the cancer? Because she got
better? But why—"

"The time for wondering is over!" Faye tossed a scrap of
white cloth over her shoulder. "We're going to the DoorWay
House. Now!"

193

Part Five

THE BRANCH

Chapter 30

The woods were a different place at night. By day, the branches seemed to stretch toward the sun. By night, they seemed to reach out toward the path, wooden fingers ready to snatch. By day, the remaining leaves were small brown hands, waving gently, whispering crinkly hellos in the wind. By night, they were black, still whispering, but darkly, warningly. And the Spanish moss that danced by day wriggled like spiders' legs, beckoned like witches' fingers by night.

Faye and Wunder didn't talk as they hurried down the path, but Davy kept up a squeaky ramble of terror.

"I don't know about this, you two," he kept saying. "I just don't know about this."

Wunder didn't know about it either, but he knew that there was nothing else to do. He couldn't put it off any longer. The questions that had been building and building for weeks—the questions he had been too afraid to ask anyone, even himself—it was time to ask them.

The sight of the house rising up beyond the live oak and the nearly bare trees, bone white in the moonlight, made Wunder shiver inside. The house seemed to tower above them, higher and higher the closer they got, all sharp points and odd angles.

There were no lights on. It was a house of shadows.

But the witch was on her porch. It was dark, so dark, but she was there. Rocking in the chair, her white clothing the only break in the blackness.

"I wasn't expecting you tonight," she said in her faraway voice. "Have you come for your letters?"

Wunder stood at the base of the porch steps. Faye was on one side of him, Davy on the other. He shook his head. "We read Mrs. Baum's," he replied. "What's going to happen on November second?"

"That," the witch said, "is up to you." She stopped rocking. "Perhaps we should go inside. Tea, I think?"

"We don't want any tea," Faye told her. "Not even one drop. We just want to know the truth."

The witch began to rock again. She considered them from her chair, her eyes two dark holes in a shadowed face.

"Did you deliver the letters?" she asked.

"Yes," Wunder said.

"And?"

"We know that they're for people who've had miracles happen to them," he said. "And also had someone they love die."

"That is a good theory," the witch said. "Although not quite correct."

"What's incorrect about it, then?" Faye demanded.

"Who has experienced a miracle?" the witch said. "Everyone. And who has lost someone? Everyone. Everyone, everyone."

This was what Wunder had been realizing as he delivered more and more letters, and as he stood in the school gym that night.

Everyone was connected to the miraculous. Everyone was connected to the dead.

But there were more questions, many more. He took a deep breath, steeled his heart, and asked, "Did you order that memorial stone—the one in the cemetery?"

"I did," the witch said. "I did."

"Why?"

The witch kept rocking. "I sit here on this porch, and what is just beyond the trees?" She gestured ahead with one hand, into the darkness. "A cemetery. For many reasons— many, many reasons—death is on my mind. I read the paper every day—"

"You read the *obituaries* every day," Faye corrected her. "We saw them on your kitchen table."

"I do," the witch agreed. "I do. I do. And there is so much death in the world. Every day, every day, every day. And so many who believe they have lost the ones they love forever. I cannot change the world. But this town, perhaps that is in my power to change." She leaned forward in the chair and her face caught the light of the moon above. She was staring right at Wunder. "The memorial stone is only the beginning of what I want to do, what I want your help to do."

"But why did you make it from Milagros?" Wunder asked. "Why did you write it that way?"

"Ah," the witch said. "You see, my name is Milagros."

She leaned back. The rocking chair began to move again, back and forth, the sound of its rails against the uneven porch planks the only noise.

Then Faye let out a scream. Davy screamed too.

"You're Milagros? That's your name?" Faye pointed a white-gloved finger at the witch. "Who are you? Who are you *really*?"

The witch sighed a long deep sigh. "That will be hard to understand. So many things in this life and after are difficult to understand. I do not know why it has to be so." She rose from the chair. "But come inside. I will explain as best I can."

"Really don't drink a single thing," Faye hissed as the witch opened the door. "What if she stole your sister's soul and she wants to steal yours? What if she's a demon? Do you have your amulet? I have mine."

"Who's stealing souls?" Davy whispered frantically. "And what about omelets? What's going on?"

Wunder didn't have his amulet, but he didn't care. He had done it—he had asked his questions at last. Whatever price he had to pay for the answers, it would be worth it.

He climbed up the porch steps and crossed to the waiting pitch-black of the open door.

He followed Milagros inside.

Chapter 31

As soon as Wunder stepped over the threshold of the DoorWay House, the stone of his heart grew not just warm but hot, began not just to shiver, but to crack.

Like it wasn't a stone at all. Like there was something inside that wanted to come out.

The witch carried a single candlestick as she led them through the house. The flame illumined only the space right around her. Outside of its glow, it was dark, dark, darker than dark. Wunder followed behind her, watching as the wall lit up one piece at a time, the bright white spirals seeming to blossom out of nothingness. He listened to the witch's footsteps, which seemed strangely slow, labored, not like the quick, graceful movements he was used to from her.

In the kitchen, the witch sat across from Wunder, Faye, and Davy. She set the candle on the table, and the flame danced up at her, lighting up the crags and cracks of her skin, making it look as though she were wearing a mask.

"This house," she said. "Do you remember what I told you this house is made of?"

"DoorWay Tree," Wunder replied. "But what we want to know—"

"DoorWay Tree," the witch continued. "And do you remember what I told you about that tree?"

"You said every town should have one. You said they can last forever. But Davy says that you—"

"That is right," the witch said, cutting him off again. "That is right. And I have been thinking, Wunder." She bowed her head forward, farther into the light. "This town . . . this town needs a DoorWay Tree. Your family needs a DoorWay Tree. So does yours, Faye. And yours, Davy. And so do I. Yes, yes, yes, so do I." The witch's black eyes met each of theirs in turn, then came back to Wunder's. "Will you get one for us?"

No one spoke. The flame flickered. This wasn't what Wunder had expected, this talk of trees. What did it have to do with the letters? What did it have to do with his sister?

"Why?" Faye finally asked. "Why do we need it? What does it do? Is it magical? Are you magical?"

"I believe," the witch said, "you asked that once before."

"And you never answered me," Faye said. "And you still haven't."

The witch leaned back, her face shadowed again, hidden. "I told you the trees are special. Their roots go down deep. Their branches reach up high. They are trees of life and trees of death, connecting worlds, connecting souls, in many ways, many mysterious ways." She nodded, as if to herself. "Yes, yes, yes, it would be good for this town to have a DoorWay Tree again. A DoorWay Tree is a marvelous thing indeed."

And suddenly the witch's request made sense to Wunder. This house, the DoorWay House, this was where it had all begun for him. This was where he had seen his first miracle, where he had become a miracologist. And this was where the witch, whoever she was, had appeared. If the house was so special, how much more powerful must the source of the house be, the DoorWay Tree?

"We'll do it," he said. "We'll get a DoorWay Tree." He could feel Faye giving him the evil eye. He could hear Davy making little noises of dissent. But he didn't care.

Time after time, he had been drawn to this house and to the witch, even when he didn't want to believe, even when he was trying to stay away. After these weeks of delivering letters, of reading *The Miraculous*, of feeling his heart telling him what his head didn't want to hear, Wunder knew he couldn't deny anymore that something was happening here, something that was too great, too overwhelming to be a coincidence.

And now the witch had promised a miracle. She had promised it in writing in a letter delivered all over Branch Hill. And Wunder believed her.

He believed in miracles again.

And if the witch needed a DoorWay Tree to do one, then he would get her a DoorWay Tree.

"We'll do it," he said again. "But how?"

The witch nodded her approval. "We are not gods," she said. "We cannot create something from nothing. We must use what exists already, change it to something new."

"So we need . . . a seed?" Wunder guessed.

The witch shook her head. "DoorWay Trees cross-pollinate, you see. That means they need each other to create seeds. But there are so few of them now, too few. Until there are more, there is only one way left to grow a new DoorWay Tree. You must plant a piece of the tree itself—a piece that connects to the trunk. A branch."

"But how can we get that?" Wunder asked. "If there are hardly any left."

"There is one I know of," the witch said. "In the town of Benedict. That is where you must go."

Faye, her wig askew, her white clothing unraveling, spoke up. "These trees," she said. "They sound pretty powerful. Pretty . . . paranormal. Who planted them?"

The witch lifted her white-cloth-wrapped shoulders once. "I don't know," she said. "I have not been so far. I know more than you, I am sure, but still very little."

"But are we allowed to plant another one?"

The witch smiled. Her perfect teeth were tiny points of brightness gleaming in the candlelight. "So much is left up to us. More than we realize, often more than we want. There was a DoorWay Tree here once, long ago. And now there will be one again. For this town. For them." She waved in the direction of the cemetery. "For me. But I am getting to be an old woman. I need help. You three, you are my help. You are my miracles. Yes, yes, yes. You are my miracles."

Chapter 32

In the end, they all said yes. And on Sunday morning, early, early, early, Wunder snuck out of his house for the second time in his life.

This time he left a note taped to the front door:

> *Went to help Davy deliver papers.*
> *Be home tonight.*

It would take seven hours to get to Benedict by train and then seven hours to get back to Branch Hill, so he wouldn't be home until after dinner. He hoped his note would keep his parents from worrying or doing anything drastic like calling the police.

Then again, he wasn't entirely sure that either of them would realize he was gone.

It was still dark as he carefully wheeled his bike out of the shed. He had attached his red wagon to it the night before, with a duffel bag full of supplies stowed inside. Once he got to the street and started pedaling, the supplies clanked and clacked with every pedal rotation, a mobile percussion set.

Faye and Davy were waiting at the bike rack by the train platform. Train rules allowed them to bring their bikes on board, but they had decided against it. Any extra steps would attract more attention, and they wanted to be as discreet as possible.

Wunder unhooked the wagon, which he *was* bringing, from his bike. The duffel bag banged and rattled and grated.

"Wundie, what do you have in there?" Faye poked the bag. It banged and rattled and grated some more.

"Things we might need," Wunder said. "We don't know where the tree is going to be, so I brought a hammer, screwdrivers, a wrench, wire cutters, some netting, a shovel. Oh, and a saw, of course. Only a handheld one. I wanted to bring the chain saw—"

Davy let out a yelp of protest.

"Too big though," Wunder continued, ignoring him.

"Oh, I wish you had brought it," Faye said. "Especially if

we get caught. Nothing says innocence like a chain saw in a gym bag."

"We won't get caught."

"Listen to you, so positive," Faye said.

"I am," Wunder said. And he smiled, a small smile. Then wider and wider, until he was grinning. It felt strange. But it felt good too, like going outside after being cooped up for a long time, like breathing in fresh air.

"All right, all right," Faye said. "That's enough. Let's go get on this train that we're probably going to get thrown off of."

They crossed one set of tracks and then went up the ramp to the train platform. Wunder led them to the very end, as far from the ticket booth as they could get. They already had wristbands and tickets. The witch had produced these from one of the squeaky-hinged kitchen cabinets on Friday night. Wunder had wondered how long she'd had them and how she had gotten them, but he hadn't asked. He had asked about other things though.

"You know, there are rules about kids traveling on trains," he had said. "We're supposed to have a parent bring us to the station and talk to the station agent."

"Yes, yes, yes," the witch had said. "It would be easier if you were older. What I am asking you to do, it will be difficult. But not impossible, I don't think. Not impossible."

They had to wait only a few minutes before their train pulled up, right on time. When the doors opened, they hurried on and found seats. The train car was empty.

The conductor came around a few minutes later. She squinted down at them.

"How old are you three?" she asked. She took their tickets and squinted at each one. Then she squinted right at Davy, who shrank back in his seat. Wunder thought he probably should have handled all the tickets, being the tallest of the three. Davy looked like a third grader. "How'd you get these tickets? And what're you going to Benedict for?"

"My father lives there," Faye spoke up. She pinned her bangs back and fixed the conductor with a deadpan stare. "My mother says he's an adulterer, a heathen, et cetera, but he's my father. Last time I threatened to curse him to the seventh level of Hades, so my friends are here with me this time. They're a calming influence."

The conductor blinked a few times. Her eyes shifted over to Wunder, who gave her his best calming smile. Davy pulled his knees up to his chin and studied the floor.

"Anything else you'd like to know?" Faye asked.

"Not a thing," the conductor said. She scanned their tickets and handed them back. "But your heathen father better be at the station at Benedict to pick you three up. Those are the rules."

When she left the train car, Wunder let out a sigh of relief.

"Great job, Faye!" he cried.

"Thank you, Wundie," Faye said. "But we still have to sneak off this train. And please stop smiling like that. It's very unnerving."

"Okay, I will," Wunder promised. But he didn't stop.

"You look insane," Faye told him. "Certifiable."

"I don't think so." Davy uncurled himself. "I think he looks happy. He always used to look like that."

"Well, then he always used to look insane," Faye said.

Wunder laughed, and Faye jerked her head away from him, her expression alarmed. "Stop that," she said.

"It sounds good," Davy said.

"It doesn't," Faye said. "Don't tell him that. It sounds maniacal, and you know it."

Wunder kept grinning. All he could think was that they were doing what the witch had asked. They were getting the tree.

And then there was going to be a miracle.

The stone of his heart was rolling from side to side to side, waiting, anticipating.

211

Chapter 33

As the day wore on, the train filled and emptied, filled and emptied. Faye spent the time reading a large leather-bound volume entitled *The Book of the Divine Prescriptions*. She said it was a very secret, very ancient text that almost no one else had read, but it had a library sticker on it, so Wunder was pretty sure that wasn't true. Davy had brought some comic books. And Wunder had *The Miraculous*— dirt-flecked, leather worn, thin and gutted.

"I haven't seen that in a while," Davy said when he noticed what Wunder was reading.

"I put it in my closet," Wunder confessed. "I even tried to leave it in the graveyard. But it kept coming back to me."

"Read me one," Davy said.

Faye closed her book. "It's impossible to concentrate on the paranormal with this incessant chatter," she said. "So let's hear one of your sunshine-and-sparkles miracles, Wundie."

Over the past few weeks, Wunder had shared more from *The Miraculous* than he ever had before. And every time he shared a miracle, he felt how powerful they were. He saw how they comforted, how they connected. He knew the perfect one to share with his friends.

"Okay," he said. "Here's one. Here's one for Davy."

Miraculous Entry #893

I realized today that I've never done an entry about Davy. Davy has been my best friend since we met in day care. As babies! How miraculous is that?

It's true that I met my other best friend, Tomás, in more "miraculous" circumstances (see Entry #97). But there are all kinds of miracles. There are everyday miracles. And I guess I just realized that meeting your best friend before you can even walk is one of those.

"The one about my mom getting better is my favorite," Davy said. "But that's my second favorite." He wasn't biting his lip. He was smiling.

Wunder smiled back at him. "It's one of my favorites too." Then his smile faltered as he remembered again how just two days ago, he hadn't been friends with Davy. "I really am sorry about how I was. Before."

Davy shrugged. "It's okay, Wunder. You were sad. I'm still your friend. I'll always be your friend."

"Wundie. David." Faye's voice was slow but very, very loud. "We get it."

Wunder turned to Faye. "You're my friend too, Faye," he said. She flipped her hood up over her head. "I hope you know that. Without you, I would never have figured out about the memorial stone and I would never have gone to see the witch and I would never—"

"Wundie! Enough!" Faye yelled, her voice shrill and deafening even through the hood. "I'm your friend too. Now read us another miracle. Something about people coming back from the dead. I think we need some more information on how that traditionally works."

So Wunder read about Lazarus. Then he read about Bodhidharma and about the daughter of the centurion and about a woman from Mississippi who was dead for three days and then sat up in her coffin at her own funeral and asked for some sweet tea. He read about holy men who were taken up into the sky and saints who climbed out of their graves and how all of nature was reborn each spring. Every time he thought there were no more dead-coming-back-to-life entries, he would turn the page and find another. As it turned out, *The Miraculous* was full of resurrections.

Faye and Davy were a good audience. They asked questions and gasped at the right parts and said, "Next!" after each one. And as Wunder read, he felt more and more like he used to, like the miracles he was telling them were true, like the miracles he was telling them were proof that the world was full of love and full of mystery, a mystery that he was a part of, a mystery that never ended.

Almost like he used to, but not quite. He knew now that wasn't the whole story. He knew there was more: darker things, painful things. But for that time, on the train, on the way to get the branch from the DoorWay Tree, all he was thinking about was the miraculous.

Chapter 34

When they reached Benedict, they rushed off the train before the conductor could come and escort them to Faye's father who, of course, would not be there. The tool-filled wagon clang-clanked as they raced through the station.

"We made it!" Wunder cried as they burst through the doors and into early-afternoon sunshine. The train station was located in what looked like the center of the town. There was a library and a post office and a large stone town hall in front of them, then lines of shops. There were a lot of people too, going in and out of these places.

"Great, we made it," Faye said. "Now what?"

"Now," Wunder replied, "we have to get the branch from the tree."

"Obviously," Faye said. "So where is it?"

Wunder shrugged, absolutely undeterred. "Let's start looking."

"Hey, Wunder?" Davy said.

Faye stared at Wunder. "What do you mean"—she grinned goofily and shrugged her cloak-covered shoulders—"'let's start looking'! You don't *know*?"

"How could I know?" Wunder asked, a little less cheerfully. "I've never been here before; have you? Maybe I should have called the mayor of Benedict and asked? Or come yesterday and scoped things out for us?"

"Wunder? Faye?" Davy said.

Faye swung her cloak back and stuck her finger in Wunder's direction. "This is a *town*, Wundie," she said. "A whole town. And we're looking for one little tree."

"It's not little," Davy said.

"How would you know, David?" Faye demanded, whirling toward him.

"Because," he squeaked, hunching into himself. Keeping his arms tucked by his sides, he pointed one finger. "Look."

Davy was pointing past the town hall, past the shops, at the very end of the main street. There was a small white building there—a church, Wunder realized, with a white bell tower and black doors. And just behind it—and above

217

it—was something he couldn't believe he hadn't seen right away.

A DoorWay Tree.

Davy was right; it wasn't little, not at all. It was tall—toweringly, sky-scrapingly tall. And its wood was black, as black as the woods on a moonless night, as black as the witch's hair, as black as death. It didn't have leaves, not one. But what it had were thousands and thousands of bright white blossoms.

Wunder started toward the tree, pulling the wagon behind him.

But he had gone only a few steps when the doors of the church swung open and people began streaming out.

"Oh, perfect," Faye said. "There are a million people here. What are we supposed to do? Lumberjack it up in front of a live audience?"

"We'll figure something out," Wunder told her. "It's going to be fine."

Faye frowned at him. "I'm really glad you've found your can-do attitude again, Wundie, but this is a serious problem."

"As soon as everyone leaves the church," Wunder said, "this whole place will be emptied out and we can get to work."

Davy trembled. Faye waved her gloved hand in irritated dismissal.

They found an out-of-the-way bench on the side of the library. They could see the church from there. And they could see the tree. Wunder was too excited to get out *The Miraculous* again, and Faye was too grumpy and Davy too tense to listen anyway. So they sat and watched and ate the peanut butter sandwiches and apples that Wunder had packed.

The afternoon ticked away, and temperatures began to drop. Faye and Davy took turns warming up in the library, but Wunder stayed on the bench. He didn't want to miss their chance. A steady stream of people continued coming and going—to get groceries, to visit the shops that sold things like ice cream and used books and handmade art. Benedict, it seemed, was a livelier place than Branch Hill.

"We're just going to have to wait until it gets dark," Wunder said as sunset grew closer and closer.

"Dark?" Davy shook his head in disbelief. "We're going to chop down a tree in the dark?"

"Not a tree. A branch, David," Faye said. "And we don't have any other choice."

"The last train to Branch Hill leaves at 8:15," Wunder said. "As long as we make that, we'll be okay."

"We won't get back to the station until three!" Davy cried. "Do you know what my mother will do to me if I come home at three in the morning?"

Wunder didn't know exactly, but he knew it wouldn't be pleasant. Mrs. Baum—cancer survivor, attorney-at-law, marathon runner—was not a woman to be trifled with.

"Call her and tell her you're staying at my house," Wunder suggested.

"She doesn't know where I am *now*," Davy said. "She's probably already so angry. If I call her, she's going to go crazy!"

"Lucky for me," Faye said, "my mother probably isn't worried at all."

Wunder wasn't sure what his parents would be thinking. He wondered if his mother had come out of her room today. He wondered if his father had been angry that he had skipped church yet again. Maybe they were relieved that he was gone. Maybe they had closed the door of his bedroom so they wouldn't have to see his bed or Milagros's crib, so they wouldn't have to think about either of them. Maybe that was what they wanted.

"It's going to work out," he said loudly. "We've made it this far. We're going to do it."

Chapter 35

At seven thirty, it was dark and cold and the town of Benedict was finally still. The stores had been closed for a few hours. An evening service ended and churchgoers headed home. Soon after, the lights inside the church turned off.

"Now!" Wunder said, jumping up from the bench.

He half ran down the block of shops, pulling the wagon as smoothly as he could to keep the clanging to a minimum. He could hear Faye's cloak flapping in the wind behind him, and he suddenly wished he had one of his own, if only for moments like these when things were dangerous and wild and exciting. A cloak, he was sure, would amplify those feelings at least a hundredfold.

At the back of the church, they came face-to-face with the DoorWay Tree for the first time.

The tree was inside a black wrought-iron fence. The fence enclosed a small plot of land that was dotted with gleaming marble and rough gray stone and glistening gold and shining silver and one statue of a majestic white bird.

The tree was in a graveyard.

"Of course," Wunder said aloud. "Where else would it be?"

The fence was short enough that Wunder was able to throw his bag to the other side and then scramble over himself. Davy needed a boost, and Faye's cloak got stuck and nearly ripped, but soon they were in the graveyard.

Despite its towering height, the DoorWay Tree's branches came down low. They spread out almost as wide as the tree was tall, swooping down, ambling back up, twisting and tangling in one another. The tree was a maze of limbs, a labyrinth of winding ways that finally joined together at the great, gnarled trunk.

Even so, the branches were too high for Wunder to reach from the ground.

"I should have brought a ladder," he said in frustration after trying and failing to climb the trunk for the tenth time.

"Too late for shoulds, Wundie," Faye told him. "Climb on David's shoulders."

"What? No!" Davy cried. "Wunder's bigger than me! And I don't want him using a saw above my head!"

"You think I do?" Faye replied.

Wunder kept trying. They couldn't have come this whole way for nothing. There had to be something they could do. But the fence wasn't close enough to the tree, and the eaves of the church roof were too far from it, and his fingertips barely brushed the lowest branch when he jumped.

"Use that gravestone!" Faye shrieked suddenly.

"Shhh!" Davy shushed her.

She was pointing at the bird statue. It was white and shining in the starlight, almost glowing. It seemed ethereal to Wunder. It seemed holy. There was no way he could stand on it.

"It's the only way," Faye said. "The dead person won't care." She bent down and shone her flashlight on the stone. "Ashley Bride will understand. We need this branch!"

"But the bird," Wunder said.

"The bird?" Faye cried. "The bird? You think the bird cares? If anything, the bird wants you to do this! It was that deranged bird dive-bombing you that started all this anyway, right?"

And somehow, that was exactly what Wunder needed to

hear. The bird was on his side. Ashley Bride was on his side. He was going to do this.

He climbed onto the outstretched wing tips of the bird statue. From there, he could reach one of the low limbs of the DoorWay Tree. He swung up onto it, and then wriggled backward until he came to a forked place. The branches were thick there. He hoped he could cut through one.

"Hand me the saw," he said.

"Be careful!" Davy had his hands pressed to his mouth as Faye passed it up.

The tree's bark was smooth underneath him, smoother than any bark he had ever felt, and it was warm too, in spite of the low temperature. The flowers surrounding him were so white that they seemed to glow, and the wind blowing through their petals sounded like a whisper.

The DoorWay Tree felt so alive.

"I hope this won't hurt, Tree," Wunder whispered. "But even if it does, you'll grow back. And this piece of you will grow somewhere else, somewhere new. I promise."

Then he started to saw.

As hard as the wood beneath him felt, Wunder didn't have much trouble starting the cut. He took this as a good omen. The tree, he thought as he worked, was willing to give up this branch. The tree wanted him to have the branch.

Things were going according to plan again. Everything was going their way. He had sawed through half of the branch, and they were going to make it back to the train in time.

Then a light turned on in the church.

"Hurry! Saw! Saw! Saw!" Faye hissed.

Wunder hurried, but his hands were sweaty now and his grip kept slipping. His arms were getting tired. The branch was so thick and the wood didn't seem to be giving under his saw the way it had at the beginning.

"Someone's coming!" Davy was whisper-screaming. "Someone's coming!"

Wunder heard a door shut somewhere on the other side of the church. He bent toward the branch, pushing back and forth, back and forth as fast as he could.

"Someone's coming, someone's coming, someone's coming." Davy was chanting this now in a high, petrified voice.

"David's right, Wundie," Faye whispered. "We've got to go."

"Almost there," Wunder said. "Come on, Tree. I need your help."

And then the branch finally broke loose. It crashed toward the ground, narrowly missing the bird statue. Davy let out a true scream—sharp and earsplitting. The someone who was coming, a man, yelled, "Who's out there?"

225

Wunder leaped to the ground. There was no reason to be quiet now.

"Everyone grab the branch!" he shouted.

Even with the three of them working together, the branch was heavy and bulky and nearly impossible to lift. They had to heave it over the fence, then load it into the wagon with frantic hands. There wasn't room for the bag of tools, so Wunder left it behind. He knew his father wouldn't be happy about that, but he couldn't help it.

As they were racing off—Wunder pulling the wagon as fast as he could and Faye and Davy steadying the branch—Wunder saw the silhouette of a man coming slowly, cautiously around the corner of the church. He didn't yell after them though. He stood and watched as they ran farther and farther away.

Chapter 36

It was 8:10 when they reached the train station, sweating and out of breath and pulling a ten-foot-long branch in a kids' red wagon.

So much for discretion.

"Where are you three going?" the ticket agent at the window called to them.

"Branch Hill," Wunder panted.

"Branch Hill." The agent looked down at something in front of him. "That's seven hours away. Your parents know you're getting on a train to Branch Hill?"

"Our parents live in Branch Hill," Wunder replied, trying to catch his breath and sound mature and responsible at the same time. "They bought us the tickets. And they're meeting us at the train."

"We've been here on UIPS business," Faye added.

"Is that some kind of gardening club?" the agent asked. He was staring at the tree branch.

Wunder was surprised when it was Davy who answered. "No," he said, his voice shaky but loud and clear. "We study the miraculous."

"The miraculous?"

Wunder knew that this was it, the final obstacle. If they could get past this ticket agent and onto the train, they would be home free. "Are you a man of faith, sir?" he asked.

The ticket agent considered this, his head bobbing back and forth. "Well, I don't follow any particular religion, but yes, I'd say I'm a man of faith."

"Then you have to believe that we need this tree branch," Wunder said. "And we need it in Branch Hill."

The agent didn't answer right away. He studied Wunder and Davy and, for quite a bit longer, Faye and her cloak. He studied the branch in the wagon. Then the train whistled from somewhere nearby.

"Good luck then, I guess," he said with a shrug.

When the train pulled up, he watched as they climbed aboard. He was still watching as they pulled away.

"Can you believe that?" Wunder cried, collapsing onto a seat. "Can you believe us? We did it! We got it! Look at this thing!"

"Yeah, great," Faye said. "Now we can plant it for the witch so she can grow some kind of magical child-eating tree or harvest some kind of fruit for her spells."

"She's not a witch," Wunder said. "She's—she's—"

He stopped talking and grinned. He didn't know what she was. He didn't know who she was. But he would know soon.

The conductor came around, but this one seemed even less devoted to the welfare of her young passengers. She didn't ask questions, just checked their wristbands and marked their tickets. They ate the last of their sandwiches and apples and some jelly beans that Faye found stashed in one of her many pockets, as the train chugged toward Branch Hill. After a few hours, Faye and Davy fell asleep, Davy leaning on Faye's cloaked shoulder.

Wunder didn't sleep. He watched the dark world blurring past his window. He thought about the houses they were passing, the people who were surely asleep as the hour grew later and later. He thought about the lives that were being lived just outside that piece of glass, and the lives that had ended in those very same places. He thought about the pain and the love that was unfolding all over, all around him, everywhere, everywhere. Even inside himself.

And he wondered what would happen when he planted the branch. He wondered what the witch's miracle would be.

He fell asleep, only for a minute. And he had a dream.

In his dream, he dug a hole on Branch Hill, in front of the memorial stone, its silver words glinting in the moonlight. He stood the branch up in the hole. It rose high above his head, white flowers swaying in the night breeze.

But then instead of growing, the branch began to shrink, smaller and smaller and smaller. Flowers fell to the ground. Little branches pulled back in until there were only four sticking out, each one ending in a cluster of tiny twigs. A wooden knot swelled at the top of the branch. A hole opened there and a cry came out.

It was a baby. A DoorWay Tree baby. It was Milagros.

"'Behold!'" the baby said, and her voice sounded soft and far away. "'Behold! I tell you a miracle. We will not all sleep, but we will all be changed'!"

"Now arriving at Branch Hill station," said the voice over the intercom.

Wunder sat up. Faye and Davy were getting to their feet. They were home. They had done it. They had actually done it.

Then the train door opened.

And Officer Soto was standing on the other side.

Chapter 37

Faye had been wrong about her mother. As soon as Officer Soto stopped in front of her house, Mrs. Lee came running out. She went right to Faye, grabbed her, and hugged her tight. Then she pushed her away to arm's length, gave her a little shake, and pulled her close again. Officer Soto drove away before Wunder could see if Faye hugged her back.

Mrs. Baum did not hug Davy. She was waiting at the curb in front of his house, arms crossed. When they pulled up, she marched over to the police car and opened the door herself.

"Out, David Baum," she ordered.

"See you, Wunder," Davy said. He looked miserable as he climbed out of the car. But then he popped his head back in and smiled. "We did it," he said, before his mother dragged him away.

Then they were at Wunder's house. No one was waiting at the curb. No one came running out the front door. Officer Soto walked him inside.

Where he found his parents. Both of them.

For the first time, Wunder wanted to be alone in his room.

His mother had been sitting on the couch, but when he came in, she got to her feet. Her dark hair was unwashed and uncombed. She was wearing an old T-shirt and sweat-pants, and her eyes had rings under them. She started toward him, then stopped. She didn't seem to know what to do with herself.

"Wunder!" she said. "Where have you been?"

"It's all right, Mrs. Ellis," Officer Soto told her. "I picked them up at the train station. And they did have that tree branch, like the ticket agent said."

"We've been so worried," Wunder's mother said. Her voice wasn't her normal voice. It had so many edges, sharp and jagged. A broken voice. "How could you—what is going on with you? First breaking into the town hall, now this! Do you think we don't have enough to worry about right now?"

Wunder's father came over and gave him a hug. Then he said, very seriously, "What did you think you were doing, Wunder? Sneaking out of the house and traveling all that way—don't you realize how dangerous that was? Where did you even get the money for the tickets? And what's going on with the tree branch?"

Wunder didn't know what to say. He had been so sure that everything would go according to plan, that his parents would find out about everything—the witch, the letters, the branch—but on the second of November. On the morning of the miracle. On that morning, he was sure that his mother would smile and hug him and his father would stay around for the whole day and the world would be changed again— this time for the better.

But things were not working out that way.

"I needed the branch," he finally said. "It's for something. For somebody."

"Who?" his mother demanded.

"You don't know her," Wunder said evasively. "She's new in town."

"Is it the old lady?" Officer Soto said. "The one living in the DoorWay House?"

234

Wunder's eyes opened wide. He knew he should deny it, but he was so surprised that he said, "How do you know about her?"

"She's our newest resident," the officer said. "And we've had some . . . concerns." He paused. "Mostly from people visiting the cemetery. It seems she invites, well, funeral attendees in. She's been sending letters too—or having them delivered, anyway." He raised his eyebrows at Wunder. "Some people felt like maybe she was spying on them or planning to—to coerce them into giving her money or something. I don't know."

"And is she?" Wunder's mother asked. "Is she spying on people and trying to get their money?"

Officer Soto shrugged. "Well, I don't know about that. We've been trying to determine if she has any legal right to be in the DoorWay House, but the records from that far back are a mess. And she's very old. I think she's probably just lonely."

"But you don't know that," Wunder's mother pressed.

"No," Officer Soto said. "I don't know that." He cracked his knuckles, one side, then the other. "And when I spoke with the police chief in Benedict, he did say there have been other attempts to take branches from that same tree. Apparently, it's very rare and it's worth a lot of money."

"Did she tell you why she wanted the tree branch, Wunder?" Wunder's father asked.

Wunder didn't say anything. Officer Soto's words were playing back in his head—*she invites funeral attendees in*. How many? he wondered. Everyone? All the friends and families of the dead that she read about in the obituaries?

"Did she ask you to do anything else, Wunder?" Wunder's mother asked.

Wunder thought about the letters, the dozens of letters he had delivered. Was that what the letters were for? Was she planning to ask for money on the second of November? And the DoorWay Tree? Was she going to sell the branch?

He shook his head.

"You need to look into this," Wunder's mother said to Officer Soto. "This old woman—it sounds like she's preying on grieving families. She's got some sort of—of mental issue. A sociopath maybe."

"We're definitely addressing the issue," Officer Soto assured her. "But, like I said, I think she's a lonely old woman who doesn't mean any harm. It's probably best if the kids stay away from her though."

"That's not good enough!" Wunder's mother was yelling now. "This woman is luring bereaved, heartbroken children to a condemned house and convincing them to commit crimes for her! What would she have asked them to do next? Steal from us? Break into a store? Vandalize the cemetery?"

"Austra, please," Wunder's father said, his voice calm but a strained, forced kind of calm. "I'm sure Officer Soto knows how to do his job."

Officer Soto looked uncomfortable. "I know you're concerned," he said. "But, well, Wunder was having problems before. It's not the first time I've had to come to your house."

This wasn't what Wunder's mother wanted to hear. She started yelling again. She started to cry. And that made Wunder feel terrible, but he was still trying to understand what had been said and what it meant for him. What it meant for his miracle.

"What about the tree branch?" he asked. No one heard him over the yelling. "What about the tree branch?" he shouted.

Officer Soto tried to crack his knuckles again, but nothing happened. "Well, that was a piece of public property," he said. "There are laws letting you cut down Christmas trees in certain areas and laws letting you chop trees for firewood, but there's no—you can't—" For a moment, Officer Soto's mouth moved, but no words came out. His hands opened in a what-can-I-say gesture. Then he said, "You can't chop up any tree you like. In a graveyard and everything. I have to—I'm going to have to take the tree branch. I can't do anything else."

After all that, Wunder wasn't even going to get the branch. He wasn't going to be able to give it to the witch.

But what did it matter anyway? What had he thought the branch was going to do? Why had he thought the witch wanted it? *She invites funeral attendees in . . . spying on them . . . coerce them into giving her money.*

It seemed like nothing had been what he wanted it to be. It seemed like everything had been exactly as it appeared to be.

The bird was just a bird.

The tree was just a tree.

And the witch? She was just an old woman living in an old, abandoned house.

Nothing more.

"I don't know what to tell you right now, Wunder," Wunder's mother said. "I don't know what to think. You would never have done anything like this before."

Wunder's exhaustion had caught up to him. The heaviness in the room, the weight of his mother's grief and his father's helplessness—it was all pressing against him so hard. He had tried to make things better, but everything was worse now, far worse. He didn't want to try anymore.

"I guess we've all changed," he said.

Then he went to his room, and he shut the door. He shut the door on all of them.

Part Six
QUESTIONS

Chapter 38

Wunder lay in bed that night, and everything was confusing in his heart, loud in his heart. He didn't know what to think. He didn't know how he felt.

And then he did. He knew exactly how he felt. He felt the way he had when Milagros had died. He felt like she had died all over again.

And he knew why.

He had let himself think there were miracles. He had let himself think that, somehow, his sister could come back. That she *had* come back. That he wasn't alone. That this horrible, terrible, overwhelmingly awful thing hadn't happened to him, hadn't happened to his family. But it had.

Milagros was dead. His sister was dead. She wasn't going to come back. There was no way for her to come back. Nothing he had ever believed in was true, and his family was shattered into pieces, and the world was dark, dark, dark, and there was no brightness to be found anywhere.

Miracles did not exist.

He didn't have any dreams that night. Not even one.

Wunder didn't go to school the next day. He slept in, and no one came to wake him up. He spent the day lying in bed, his face turned toward the wall. *The Miraculous* was in his backpack, and he didn't get it out.

He heard the phone ringing that afternoon and into the evening. His father was at work and his mother was almost certainly in her room, so no one answered it.

He didn't go to school on Tuesday either. He didn't stay in his room though. He spent the day biking around town. He knew someone would probably see him—after years of miracology and weeks of letter-delivering, almost everyone in town knew him by now—but he didn't care. He biked past St. Gerard's. He biked past the town hall. He biked past Safe and Sound Insurance and past the Lazar house.

He didn't go past the cemetery though. He didn't go anywhere near the woods.

He came home that afternoon, before school let out, before kids filled the streets, heading to their houses. He got enough snacks to last him the evening and then headed to his room.

But he stopped on the way there.

The door to his parents' room was open. And no one was inside.

He heard the front door close about an hour later. Then the door to his parents' room closed.

It was the first time Wunder's mother had left the house in over a month. He wondered where she had been, but he was too tired to wonder for long.

Then his father came to see him after work that evening, another first. He hadn't been in Wunder's room since Milagros was born.

"How was school today?" he asked.

Wunder shrugged. He was back in bed. He was staring at the ceiling. He was trying his best to think about nothing.

"Fine," he said.

Wunder's father stood there in the doorway with his chin in his hand. He was frowning, and Wunder was sure he was going to tell him that he knew he had skipped school. He was sure that he was angry.

But then his father looked into the corner of the room. He looked at the crib there with its white flowered sheet, still made up, still ready and waiting and waiting and waiting.

Wunder's father sighed. "Tomorrow, you have to go to school, Wunder," he said gently. "And then you have to come right home. You're grounded. For a long time."

And the next morning, he was back.

"Time to get up." He watched as Wunder sat up and swung his legs around. "I know you haven't wanted to go to church, but I was thinking we could go together on Thursday, for All Saints' Day." He paused. "Or Friday. Friday is All Souls' Day."

"I don't want to go," Wunder replied.

"Okay," his father said. "Okay. Fine. Maybe we can do something else. Together, I mean. The two of us." He glanced at the corner of the room. "There are a lot of things we need to do."

Wunder didn't answer.

At school that day, he didn't want to talk to anyone, but he especially didn't want to talk to Faye or Davy. They both kept trying to catch his eye, but he wouldn't look at them. He went to each class late and left each one early. He ate lunch in the stairwell.

Finally, in science class, Faye got up in the middle of the lesson and walked right over to him. "Wundie, we need to talk," she said.

"Faye," Ms. Shunem said. "You know I usually don't mind social interaction during this class, but not while I'm teaching. Please sit down."

"I'm sorry, Ms. Shunem," Faye said without moving. "I'm just trying to make sure that Wundie heard me."

"I heard you, Faye," Wunder said. But five minutes before the bell rang, even though Ms. Shunem was still talking, he grabbed his backpack and left the class.

He hurried down the halls, toward the front door. He didn't stop at his locker. He wanted to leave as fast as he could. He wanted to run out the school door and back to the safety of his room, where no one would talk to him about anything. He thought about locking the door too. Maybe his father wouldn't bother him if the door was locked. He didn't seem to bother Wunder's mother.

"Hey, Wunder, wait up!" It was Tomás's voice.

Wunder stopped and turned before he really thought about it. Tomás was jogging toward him. He must have left science class early too.

"My dad told me about—about what happened," Tomás said. "He wanted to know if I had anything to do with it."

"Did you tell him that we're not even friends anymore?"

Tomás looked hurt. "We're friends," he said. "We are. But with everything that happened—and you haven't been, I don't know, yourself—and I've been busy with soccer and

247

everything." He paused and flipped his hair, a gesture that suddenly looked self-conscious. "I mean, what were you doing with that tree anyway?"

Wunder searched for an answer, but his insides were a checkerboard again, and all his words had been blacked out, especially those words, words about this most recent, most raw loss.

He realized that he had been silent for a long time. Tomás was staring at him, craning his neck forward, brow furrowed, like he was trying to see if Wunder had gone comatose.

"It was for Milagros," was what he finally said.

"Milagros?"

"My sister," Wunder said. "It was for my sister. It was a mistake though."

The bell rang. Wunder left the school and headed back home to his room.

Chapter 39

Wednesday night was Halloween. Wunder stayed in his room, listening to the doorbell rings and knocks as children came for their tricks and treats. His father had asked him if he wanted to help pass out candy, but he had said no.

Then, after one of the knocks, his bedroom door opened. His father was standing there. And behind him were Davy and Faye.

Davy was wearing his rock costume again. There were holes in the trash bag with pieces of newspaper sticking through.

Faye wasn't dressed as the witch. She had on her cloak with the black dress she had worn to the funeral underneath.

Her face was expressionless as usual, but Wunder knew that she was not serene.

"You're not allowed to go out, Wunder," his father said, "but I thought you could use some company."

He left the door open, but Faye shut it firmly after him.

"Your room is very spartan," she said.

"What happened to your pictures?" Davy asked. "And your books and your statues? You got rid of everything?"

"Except that," Faye said. She pointed a gloved hand to the corner of the room. To the crib. "Why is that still in here? That's awful."

Wunder wanted them to leave. He got up from his bed. "Why are you here? You heard my dad. I can't go trick-or-treating."

"Wundie," Faye said. "We're not here about candy collecting. We know you've been avoiding us because the police took the branch, but we're not mad. We understand. What were you going to do, fight the hair-flipper's dad? But listen. You need to go see the witch. She's been asking about you."

"She's not a witch," Wunder replied.

"I know," Faye said. "She's not. I know who she is. And you do too."

"An old woman," Wunder said.

"Who she really is."

"Probably a con artist. Or a lunatic."

"What are you talking about?" Faye said. "Her name is Milagros." She held up one finger. "She showed up the day after your sister died." Another finger.

"She looks like your sister!" Davy said. "Well, like the picture I saw in the paper. Her eyes or something."

"And she asked David all those questions about you," Faye continued. "She had you deliver the letters, get the tree branch. And she—"

"The witch is not my sister!" Wunder yelled, angry that they were making him say those words, angry that they were making him even think them. "How could she be my sister? It doesn't make any sense!"

"It's a miracle, Wundie," Faye said. "It doesn't have to make sense."

Wunder shook his head. "She was using us. She was trying to see what we would do for her!"

"Now you don't make sense," Faye said.

"Officer Soto said that tree we chopped up is really rare," Wunder told her.

"Yeah, she told us that," Faye said.

"Rare and *expensive*. She just wanted to sell it!"

Davy gnawed nervously on his bottom lip. Faye stared at

251

Wunder, her face completely still, like she had been frozen. Shocked, Wunder thought. As shocked as he had been.

But he was wrong.

"Are you crazy?" Faye's words exploded, high and sharp and loud. "That's what you think? You think she was trying to run some kind of—of botanical-theft ring? That's ridiculous!"

"It's not ridiculous!" Wunder found himself shouting back. "It's the most rational explanation!"

"So what?" Faye shoved her bangs from her face. She pinned them up with fast-fingered fury. "I can't believe you're still not convinced! You really think everything that's happened is a coincidence? What about the spirals? What about the letters? Why would she tell everyone to come to Branch Hill?"

"Officer Soto said she's been inviting other people into the DoorWay House," Wunder said. "Other funeral-goers. She's probably asking them to steal things for her too. Or asking for money. Or maybe she's"—he struggled to think of another reason, a non-miraculous reason—"starting a cult."

Faye pulled her hood up. She glared at him from the shadows of its peak. "You don't believe that."

"Why not?" Wunder cried. "What has she actually done? She hasn't done anything for me! She's a—she's a fake!"

"I don't think that can be true." Davy spoke up for the first time. "When we were in her house—" He was quiet for a moment. "When my mom was sick—really sick—I would go in her room late at night sometimes. And you know we're not—we're not very religious or anything. But I would feel something in the room. Something that would make me feel better. And I felt that in the house. In the DoorWay House."

"It's what we wanted to feel," Wunder said. "That's what everything has been. She's not what we thought she was. That's just who we wanted her to be, who I wanted her to be." He crossed his arms. "I'm not going to see her. I never want to see her again."

"Well, just because you're not going back doesn't mean Davy and I have to stop!" Faye said. "If you're not going to believe in your miracle, that's fine. Maybe there will be one for me! Do you even remember my grandfather?"

Wunder stared at her. "What do you mean? I never met your grandfather."

"Do you remember that he *died*? That I was close to him? That I've been"—she pulled her hood down even farther, covering her eyes, before continuing—"that I've been sad since he died?"

"I did know that," Wunder said. "And I'm sorry. But he was old! He lived a long time! He was—"

"He wasn't old!" Faye screamed, shoving her hood back. "He was fifty-nine! He was young! He was really young to die. And he knew there were miracles at the DoorWay House. He saw the spirals spinning, just like you did, and he knew about the shadows I saw there. He would have believed that Milagros is a miracle, and I do too! She said she was going to help everyone who had lost someone. She said she was going to help me! And she's going to, I know she's going to!"

Wunder was too angry to feel bad about what he'd said. He was too angry to do anything except yell back, "She can't help anyone! It's all lies!"

Faye glared at him. Then she swung her cloak around herself. "Here you go again, Wunder," she said. "Something bad happened, so now you don't believe in anything anymore, right? Well, not me. I'm going to find my miracle. I'm not afraid of the dark."

She strode from the room. Davy stayed, biting his lip and looking torn and miserable.

"Milagros said to tell you that when you're ready, she'll be there," he said softly.

Wunder's backpack was next to his bed. He grabbed *The Miraculous* out of it. "Take this to her," he said. Then he threw the book at Davy.

Davy stepped out of the way just in time. Then he picked the book up and left.

And the stone of Wunder's heart felt colder than it ever had, heavier than it ever had.

And empty too. His heart was empty.

Chapter 40

At school the next day, Wunder didn't even have to try to avoid Faye and Davy. Davy waved at him once, but mostly he stayed next to Faye, who acted as if Wunder didn't exist. Which was fine with Wunder. He hadn't asked for any of this.

By the time he got home, he felt exhausted, which didn't make any sense. He hadn't done anything. But he went straight to his room and lay on his bed. He wondered if it had been like this for his mother, if the less she did, the less she felt able to do. If the more she was alone, the more she wanted to be alone.

He must have fallen asleep when he heard someone say, "Wunder."

He looked up to see his mother in his doorway.

Wunder jumped out of bed. Only six weeks ago—it seemed like years ago, how could it have been so recently?—having his mother in his room was nothing unusual. She was always in there, after school to sit at his desk and talk to him about his day, at night to tell him to sleep tight, on Saturday mornings to read his new *Miraculous* entries.

But now—now his first thought was that she needed to leave. Not because he was angry at her, although he was. She needed to leave because of what was in the far corner of the room.

He wondered frantically how to hide the crib, if he could throw a blanket over it or position himself in front of her somehow. He knew she wouldn't want to see it. That was why it was still in his room. The crib was a reminder of what had happened, and she did not want to be reminded.

But there was nothing he could do. She saw it right away, and she stood there, as silent as Wunder had been with Tomás, rooted in place, petrified, ossified.

When she finally spoke, her voice was loud and tight sounding, spooled-up sounding. "Dad has to work late tonight. And I have to go out for a little while. I have something to do. Please don't go anywhere."

Then she turned and almost ran from the room. Wunder

went to the hall and watched as she fled out the front door, slamming it behind her. She hadn't stopped to change from her slippers into her shoes. She hadn't brought her coat. She hadn't even taken her keys.

Wunder stayed in the hallway, watching the door, waiting for her to come back in. She didn't, but he couldn't bring himself to go back into his room. It was suddenly the last place in the world he wanted to be.

It was less than an hour later that the doorbell rang.

Wunder was sure it must be his mother, keyless and cold. He went to the front door and opened it.

But it wasn't his mother on the other side.

Standing on the porch was Officer Soto.

"Hey there, Wunder," the officer said.

"Oh. Hello," Wunder said.

Officer Soto wasn't wearing his uniform. He was wearing jeans and an old blue letterman jacket from Oak Wood High School. The patch on the front showed an oak tree. Two of the branches, spreading up and out, ended in hands. Wunder knew it was supposed to look like the tree was about to catch a football, but there was no football on the jacket. It looked, to him, like the tree was reaching up toward a blue sky.

"You don't have to invite me in," Officer Soto said. "I can

talk to you right here for a minute." He cracked his knuckles. *Pop, pop, pop*, they went, like little exclamations, little bursts of emotion leaving him. "Sure is weird to see you without a smile."

Wunder waited. Whenever he saw Officer Soto lately, there was bad news. He wondered what the bad news would be this time.

"Tomás told me that the tree—" Officer Soto said. "Well, he told me that you wanted the tree for—well, for your sister. He said that maybe the old woman wanted it too, but that really it was for you and your sister and he thought I oughta—" The officer paused. He tried to crack his knuckles again, but they were already popped. "Well, I know—I know things have been tough for you. For your parents too. When my dad died—" He paused again. "Well, that thing's been sitting in my office for days. It's starting to fall apart. And I thought—you weren't planning on selling it or anything, were you?"

Wunder shook his head slowly, cautiously. "No, sir," he replied.

"And you're not going to give it to the, uh, the DoorWay House lady, are you?"

Wunder shook his head again.

"Well, then, anyway, there's no reason I can see that you

can't—I mean, no charges were filed, so it's not evidence. Benedict didn't ask for it back or anything. And after everything you kids went through to get it . . . Well, we were just going to throw it away. So . . ."

"You're going to let me have it?" Wunder asked, even though he knew he shouldn't. Officer Soto seemed to be trying very hard to not say exactly that.

The officer shrugged. "Well, you know," he said.

He turned to leave. And Wunder knew that he should let him leave, he shouldn't push things, not with all the trouble he'd been in, all the trouble he'd caused. And anyway, he didn't care, but he found himself asking, "Have you heard anything else about the witch—I mean, about the old woman? The DoorWay House woman?"

Officer Soto shook his head. "She's been real quiet there. We've been keeping an eye on her, doing a patrol past the house every now and then. Had to tell your friend—the one with the cape thing?"

"Faye," Wunder said.

"Yeah," Officer Soto said. "Had to tell her to leave yesterday. She called me 'Officer Mundane.' Said I was an agent of the banal and humdrum. Sort of screamed it at me, actually."

Wunder nodded. "That sounds like her."

"Well, anyway, there it is." He gestured toward the other end of the porch, where Wunder now saw the tree branch had been all along, leaning against the house, listening as its fate was decided. "Like I said, do what you want with it, but don't give it to the DoorWay House lady. That wouldn't look good—you know, for me. And anyway, it's for your sister, right? Whatever you were planning to do with it, do that. For her."

Chapter 41

Wunder sat on the porch for a long time after Tomás's dad left. He sat on the porch and stared at the tree branch. Against the white wood of the house, the branch looked dark, but it wasn't the deep black it had seemed in Benedict. It was duller, a charcoal-gray color. Its flowers were gone. Its bark was a rough, peeling patchwork and beneath it, Wunder could see the spiraling grain.

He sat and stared at the tree branch as evening turned into night. Its wood grew darker and darker. Its spirals grew lighter and lighter.

They didn't spin though. Of course they didn't.

Wunder thought about what he'd told Tomás, about what

Officer Soto had said—that the branch was for his sister. And it was true. He had wanted the tree branch for Milagros, for the sister he had loved and lost so quickly. Everything he had done—breaking into the town hall and entering the DoorWay House, delivering the letters and talking with the witch and stealing the branch—it had all been for her.

And also for himself. He had wanted a miracle so badly. He had wanted an answer, a sign. He had wanted to know that the world wasn't truly so harsh and hard, that people weren't truly so alone, that everything didn't truly end so abruptly and awfully and heartbreakingly.

And he thought about the last entry in *The Miraculous*. The entry that he had not wanted to read or think about. He didn't have *The Miraculous* anymore; who knew what Davy had done with it.

But it didn't matter. He knew what the last entry said:

Miraculous Entry #1306

I was alone with her yesterday, with Milagros. She has her own room here at the hospital, and usually we're all in it—me and Mom and Dad—but today Dad convinced Mom to have coffee with him in the hospital café. Mom wasn't going to go—she never wants to leave Milagros—but she finally agreed when I told her I would watch her. I told her I'd keep my sister safe.

Milagros was sleeping in the incubator—that's this plastic box with a cover to keep her warm—and there were all these machines around it. I was watching her, and she kept making these jerky movements. Her little arms would fly open and her whole body would sort of shudder, like someone was scaring her. And her little hands kept opening up and then squeezing shut like she wanted to hold on to something.

And I knew I wasn't supposed to do this, but I felt like I had to—I opened one of the windows in the plastic cover. I put my hand in—it was clean, really clean, because they make you wash for two minutes when you come in. They even have picks for you to clean your nails.

And as soon as I put my finger next to her hand—she grabbed it! She grabbed my finger and she held on tight.

I don't know what I expected, but I didn't expect that. I didn't expect a baby to be that strong. Especially not a baby who everyone says is so sick. Especially not a baby who everyone says is going to die.

And then she opened her eyes, so big and round and dark—and she looked right at me.

And I'd been waiting to feel it, I'd been waiting since she was born, and I felt it then. With just the two of us there, holding hands and looking at each other, I felt the heart-bird.

There's going to be a miracle. I'm sure of it.

He had waited for the miracle.

But it had never come.

Unless it had.

The night was dark. The tree limb was black. Everything was quiet.

Wunder got up. He was going to see the witch.

Chapter 42

Wunder ran toward the woods. He ran as fast as he could, ducking behind cars and trash cans whenever he saw headlights coming his way. He didn't want to be seen. He didn't want to be asked questions. He didn't want to explain himself. He just wanted to find out, once and for all, the whole truth.

It was a gusty night, and over the sound of his own footfalls Wunder could hear the long drawn-out rumbles of a brewing autumn storm. The wind seemed to push him forward. The thunder sounded like a low, faraway voice whispering words he couldn't quite catch.

He didn't hesitate when he reached the edge of the

woods, but his breath caught in his throat as he plunged in. The wind was howling there, rushing down the paved path and through the now-bare trees, making everything not only shiver and wave, but shake and whip. His feet crunched over the debris that littered the path—dry leaves and displaced Spanish moss and whole branches that had come crashing down. And once he rushed past the live oak, once he was on the dirt trail, there were no leaves or vines blocking his view. He could see straight through to the DoorWay House.

Where, for the first time since before the funeral, the witch was not on the porch.

The house was dark. Not a single light was on. The windows that weren't broken shone black, blank in the light of the waning crescent moon. Even the spirals on the house seemed darker than usual.

Wunder wasn't running anymore. His breath came in shuddering gasps as he crept over to the house and then up the stairs to the porch. For so long, this place had seemed so wondrous to him—magical, sacred, otherworldly. It was the place where he had begun to believe, truly believe in miracles.

And now here he was, climbing the splintered, spiraled stairs of the DoorWay House in the dead of night. Here he was, with the stone of his heart cracking and splitting, then stilling and hardening. Here he was, having buried a sister and spoken with a witch. Here he was, having stolen and lied and spent hour after hour in a cemetery where the dead seemed gone, gone forever. Here he was, having learned the pure loves and deep sorrows of Branch Hill, having questioned the truths of life and death, having connected the dots of hundreds of souls.

And what did he believe now?

He didn't know, he didn't know.

But here he was.

At the door, he hesitated for a moment. Then he turned the doorknob.

Caw! A bird's cry sounded over the noise of roaring wind and thrashing branches and rushing dead leaves. *Caw!*

Wunder stepped over the threshold and into the waiting pitch-black of the DoorWay House.

The vacillations of his heart only intensified inside the house. It made Wunder want to wrap his arms around himself, to try to hold himself together, but he couldn't. He needed his hands, because there was no light. He moved forward with cautious shuffles, arms outstretched, the floor-to-ceiling spirals that usually sent him reeling hidden in the blackness.

He knew, only from memory, when the hallway ended. A few steps later, his hand hit something hard, and a noise, discordant and growling, sounded out. He spun toward the door before he realized what it was—the piano in the parlor. He put his hands out again. He kept on, farther and farther into the darkness.

In the dining room, he held on to the wooden table, letting it guide him to the doorway at its end. And it was there that he finally saw the light, just a pinprick at first.

Then a glow.

Then a radiating halo.

And in the center of it, the face of the witch.

Chapter 43

The witch was sitting at the table in the kitchen, a candle in front of her. In the flickering light, her hair looked gray. Her face looked crumpled and sunken, like a mummy's, like a corpse's.

"You have come," she said in her faraway, low voice.

"I'm here," Wunder said. His voice was high and quavering. Now that he was here, he was afraid of what might happen. Now that he was here, he wished he hadn't come.

"You are the last one," the witch said. "I have your invitation."

She took an envelope from the white cloth that shrouded

her and held it out to him with hands that seemed to tremble.

Wunder took the letter in both hands. It was the same as the others but with his name instead of someone else's. He traced the tree on the wax seal, the DoorWay Tree. His fingers moved down the roots and then up the branches, to the flowers.

When he looked back up, the witch was watching him intently through her black eyes.

"You have something to say, Wunder," she said. "Yes, yes, yes. Tell me what you have come to say."

Wunder felt like he had when he went to see Mariah Lazar, certain that he was at the end, certain that he was about to learn everything he so desperately longed to know, everything he was so utterly terrified to know.

Only instead of asking question after question, he couldn't seem to get even one out.

"If you're not her," he finally said, "if you're not my sister, then you're a terrible person. A horrible, terrible person. It's not right to do what you're doing."

"What do you think I am doing?" the witch asked.

"I don't know," Wunder said. "I don't know what you're doing. Officer Soto said—my mother thinks—"

"Whatever your mother thought," the witch said, "she

271

does not think anymore. She has come to visit me twice now. In fact, she left just before you arrived."

Wunder stared at her, stared straight through the light and into the dark of her eyes. "My mother? My mother came here?"

The witch nodded once. "Yes, yes, yes. She is very worried about you."

"She's not." Wunder shook his head. "She's not worried about me at all."

"She is," the witch said. "And she had many questions to ask."

Questions. Wunder thought of his mother here, in this kitchen, and he realized what it meant. His mother, who had been so paralyzed by grief that she had hardly left her room in weeks, his mother who had fled the house shoeless at the sight of his sister's crib—his mother had been with the witch.

The witch who read the obituaries and spoke about the dead. The witch whose name was Milagros.

The witch who Faye and Davy were convinced was Wunder's dead sister.

"What did you tell her?" His voice was suddenly loud, hard, the shakiness gone. "Did you tell her your name? Did you tell her who you are? What did you say to her?"

The witch smiled, a sad smile. "I gave her an invitation, and I answered what she was ready to ask. But some things—some things can never be said. Some miracles must be understood without words."

Wunder felt the stone of his heart go horribly still at this, go cold at this, cold as the grave, cold as death.

"There are no miracles!" he cried, his words both a challenge and a plea to the witch to prove him wrong.

The witch moved back from the light. In the shadows, she pressed her fingers to her temples. "How to explain it?" Her voice seemed to have grown softer, farther away, but it was heavier too, weighed down. "All around us are miracles. Most are marvelous and wonderful and bright and so clearly seen. But not all. Because there can be miracles even in the midst of unfathomable sadness and anger, even in the depths of grief and confusion. And these, these are the hidden ones, the ones we must search for."

"The minister isn't searching for miracles," Wunder told her. "Neither is Eugenia Simone. And neither is my mother."

"Maybe they weren't," the witch said. "But after talking to you, they may feel differently. A long-loved wife recovering from an illness, even if only for a short time; a family saved from a fire; two tiny babies coming into this world to stay: You reminded so many in this town of their miracles, bright

273

and shining. And you have also begun to show them the hidden miracles, the ones that are so hard to see, the ones that are so often forgotten: the never-ending memory of a cherished one; the hands of friends, new and old, reaching out to hold you up; the love you give, the love you receive, even when that love comes from someone you cannot see or hear. Wunder, even in death there are miracles, for the living and for the dead."

"Then why did you want the DoorWay Tree?" Wunder demanded. "You said the town needed it. You said the dead needed it. If death is so miraculous, why does anyone need help? Why do you need help?"

The witch smiled her sad, sad smile. "Because sometimes all that we can understand isn't enough. It is easy to see the beautiful in happy times. It is easy to reach for one another in the brightness. But so many things get lost, lost in time, lost in the dark spaces between sorrows. That's what the DoorWay Tree is for, what it has always been for. The roots of the tree reach deep down into the earth, and the branches of the tree reach high up into the sky. The tree is a way to bring the hidden miracles into the light, to connect us, to show us what has been there all along."

Wunder shook his head. "It's just a tree," he said. "Nothing more. What can a tree do?"

"All that it was meant to do," the witch said. "The dead are not gone, Wunder. The living are not alone. This world is not all there is. There is more, yes, yes, yes, there is more. But sometimes we need help to see these mysteries, to reach beyond our sorrow, beyond time, beyond death. Just as a tiny hand reached out to you, reached out and held on so tight."

When the witch said this, Wunder felt as if there was a pressure on his pointer finger. He looked down, sure he would find four small fingers and a thumb wrapped around it.

But there was nothing.

There was only the witch, watching him from across the table with her black eyes.

"Who are you?" he whispered to her. "What do you want with me? What do you want with us, with all of us?"

"Only to help," she said. "Only to show you—" She stopped and pressed her temples again. She shook her head slowly, back and forth. "Maybe it is wrong, maybe it is more than I am allowed, but I couldn't go on without doing this. You may not understand, but I want you to believe—I want you to believe that there are miracles."

"I don't," Wunder said. He was holding on to his right

pointer finger with his left hand, squeezing it as if to stanch blood flowing from a cut. The stone of his heart was so heavy and so cold and his thoughts were spiraling, and he didn't understand, and it wasn't enough. "I don't believe in anything!"

He fled from the room, fled into the darkness. He could hear the witch behind him, calling his name—"Wunder, Wunder, Wunder"—but her voice had grown so soft that it was only a whisper, a faint sound that the pounding of his feet covered up.

He was going so fast that he crashed into the dining room table. He struggled back to his feet and kept going. Through the parlor and into the hall where, off balance, he careened into walls that he could not see.

Outside, the weather had grown even wilder, the winds gusting even more strongly. Rain poured down and thunder cracked, close now. If the bird was still cawing, Wunder could not hear it over the storm.

He ran past the DoorWay House sign and down the dirt trail. He ran down the paved path and back into the neat row of homes that bordered the woods. The streetlamps were on there. The world looked so ordinary.

He stopped under a light and he took out the envelope. The rain turned his name into a blurry gray puddle, then erased it entirely as he opened the flap and removed the letter:

"Behold! I tell you a miracle. We will not all sleep, but we will all be changed."

Come to the highest point of Branch Hill Cemetery at sunrise on the second of November. In this place of remembrance and love, we will experience miracles, and we will all be changed. Together.

It was the same as the other letters. Exactly the same. Except for two words, scrawled at the bottom.

For Milagros.

Wunder put the paper, now soft and soaked, back into the envelope. He put the envelope into the pocket of his jeans.

He walked back on the main street. He didn't care if anyone saw him.

When he got home, he climbed the stairs to the porch. He dragged the DoorWay Tree branch down the porch steps and to the side of the house. His bicycle was leaning there. The wagon was there too, the rope still hanging from its handle. His father had picked both up from the police station.

Wunder tied the wagon to the bicycle. Then he hoisted the branch into it, first one end and then the other.

Then he started to pedal back down the street.

Back toward the woods.

Back toward the DoorWay House.

Back to the cemetery.

Part Seven

THE TREE

Chapter 44

At the cemetery, Wunder flung open the black iron gates, then rode through them. He rode up the paved path, rode as far as he could, until he came to the base of Branch Hill.

Then he got off his bike. He pushed one end of the tree branch from the wagon, then lifted the other end. He started up the hill, dragging the limb along behind him.

He didn't have a shovel. The shovel was in the duffel bag along with his father's other tools that had never made it back from Benedict. The earth was hard at the top of the hill, but the rain had softened it. He pressed his hands into the mud and began to dig.

It was hard work because for every handful of dirt he scooped out, the rain washed some back in. But he didn't stop. Down into the earth his hands went, down and down and down, until he had a hole that he thought would do.

Now the tree branch seemed even heavier. He wrestled one side into the hole, then put his hands under the other end and pushed up. But his fingers slipped and the branch came crashing to the ground.

He bent down again. He wrapped both arms around the branch and pulled it close. Then he lifted it up, all the way up this time, and he settled it down, the branch of the Door-Way Tree, down into the earth.

Into the earth that held the dead. Into the earth that held Florence Dabrowski and Quincy Simone and Avery Lazar and Faye's grandfather. Into the earth that held the hundreds of loved ones of the people of Branch Hill.

Into the earth that held Milagros, his sister.

He held the branch there, upright, reaching high above his head. He held on to it as tightly as he could, with all the strength he had, as the rain fell and the moon shone and the gravestones around him looked on.

And then he had to let go.

Because the branch began to spin.

It was like the world was on fast-forward, like time-lapse

photography. The branch rotated, slowly, then faster and faster, shedding its sickly gray bark. Underneath, the wood was a vibrant, dark ebony. Underneath, the spirals that covered the wood were as white as ever, as bright and light as ever. Wunder watched as the branch spun. He watched as the spirals began to spin too.

The branch grew taller, thicker—a trunk. And then limbs unfolded, as if they had been inside the whole time, waiting to stretch upward. Branches sprouted from the limbs, twigs from the branches, until there was a tangle of wood, a maze of new growth, extending out and up, high, high, higher than high. And Wunder couldn't see it, but he could feel the same thing happening under the earth, could feel the roots tunneling down deep, deep, deeper than deep.

The spirals spun.

And then came the flowers, bursting from the ends of the twigs. Pure white and startling in the darkness, they blossomed. Each one sent a jolt through Wunder, one after another, until the branches were covered, until the tree was full.

Then one flower fell.

It came floating down, coasting gently, as if on wings, petal wings, circling in tighter and tighter spirals until—

The flower landed right in Wunder's outstretched hands.

The spirals stopped spinning. The tree stopped growing. It stood there, reaching up to the sky, reaching down into the earth. It stood there as if it had always been there, as if it was right where it was supposed to be.

Here among the dead.

Here in front of a living boy.

And suddenly Wunder understood.

Everyone was connected. The living to the living, and the living to the dead, and the dead to the dead too. And no one was ever alone. And no one was ever truly gone. And nothing ever ended.

Because love never ended.

And no one knew—no one could ever know all that was happening. In this life or after.

There were truths that couldn't be measured. There were connections that couldn't be traced. There were mysteries that couldn't be unshrouded. There were ways to hold someone's hand even when that hand was buried far under the ground, even when that someone was lying in a small white box.

There was sadness, there was never-ending sadness, sadness that left you motionless in your bed, sadness that chased you away from home day after day, sadness that could make your heart feel like a stone.

But there were miracles too.

There were miracles.

At the base of the tree, there was a hole. A hollow place. Wunder found it because instead of being dark, the hole was lit, lit by a soft, pulsing white light.

He climbed inside.

There wasn't much room. He had to pull his knees up to his chest to fit. But it was warm in there. Warm and the wood at his back felt softer than he'd thought it would.

And waiting for him there was the feeling that he had felt in the DoorWay House. And something else—someone else.

She was there. He couldn't see her, couldn't touch her, but he knew she was there. The one he had been waiting and waiting and waiting for. The one he'd thought was never coming.

His sister, Milagros, was there.

And his heart, that stone that had warmed and rocked and shook and cracked, it split wide open.

Because it hadn't been a stone.

It had been an egg.

And finally, finally, the heart-bird was reborn. It burst free and soared through him, feathers brushing his veins, his heart, the insides of his fingertips and the soles of his feet. It soared and sang, and it was different—it wasn't all light and bright and lifted, there was loss and loneliness and dark-ness too—but it was beautiful all the same.

Wunder felt it. He felt it all, but he was tired. He was so tired and he ached. Not just his hands or his back, but everywhere. He ached everywhere.

And so, hidden inside the DoorWay Tree, with his cheek pressed against his knees and his arms wrapped around his shins, with the heart-bird flying and the soft light surround-ing him and the white flower clutched in his earth-covered hands, Wunder cried.

He cried and cried and cried.

Chapter 45

"Wake up, Wundie! Wake up!"

Slivers of weak gray light were filtering into the hole in the tree where Wunder was curled. The soft white light was gone, and the wood at his back was rough and hard. His limbs felt tight and heavy as he crawled out, as if he had slept for a long, long time.

Faye was there, her cloak covering a gray sweater dress. Her bangs were pinned back. She didn't look serene. She didn't look expressionless. She looked shocked and confused and a little bit afraid.

"What happened to you?" she asked. "You're covered in mud. You're—you're in a tree. A DoorWay Tree! What happened?"

Wunder staggered to his feet and turned to stare up at the tree. He could hardly believe it was still there. It wasn't possible. It wasn't rational.

But it was there.

And he knew exactly what to say.

"We did it," he told Faye.

Faye gaped at him. She pulled her cloak around herself tightly. Then she gazed up at the DoorWay Tree's delicate white blossoms, and down its black wood to the bumps and knobs of roots burrowing into earth.

"We did it," she breathed.

"I'm sorry I didn't wait for you," Wunder said.

Faye shook her head slowly, without taking her eyes off the tree. "I didn't know what would happen," she said. "I knew something would. But I didn't know what."

"You were right about Milagros," Wunder told her. "You were right about miracles."

He crossed to the lowest branch. Standing on tiptoes, he was able to pluck one of the white flowers. It felt warm in his hands even though the sun wasn't visible yet.

"This is for you," he said, holding it out to his friend.

"Wundie. Listen," Faye said. "That's sweet. But I don't really see you like that."

Wunder laughed. "For you and for your grandfather. What was his name? I'm sorry I never asked."

"Daniel," Faye told him. "Daniel Young-Ho Lee."

"For you and Daniel Young-Ho Lee," Wunder said.

Faye took the flower. Her fingertips brushed each petal, one by one, then she leaned in and inhaled. When she looked back up, she didn't seem confused or afraid anymore.

She seemed, for the first time since he'd known her, serene.

"What happened in there?" she asked, pointing to the hollow that Wunder had come out of.

"I'm not sure how to explain it," Wunder said. "But she was there. She's not really gone. Well, maybe she is. But she's—she's still here too. With me."

Faye pressed the flower to her heart, like she was giving it a hug, and she smiled.

"I knew it," she said. "I knew he wasn't gone. But I couldn't feel it before. I can feel it now."

They were silent, watching as the breeze made the white blossoms dance, watching as sunrise light shone through the thin petals, showing the veins that flowed through them, showing the blank spaces between.

Then they heard footsteps.

Someone was coming up the hill.

Chapter 46

It wasn't just someone. It was many someones—the women and men and children of Branch Hill. They had letters clutched in their hands. They had wide eyes. And they had questions for Faye and Wunder.

"The letter told us to come here," someone said.

"What's this about?"

"Who sent these?"

"Wunder! Wunder!"

At the bottom of the hill was the Minister of Consolation. He wore his white robe, and in the new sunlight, it looked bright white, as white as a DoorWay Tree flower.

"Wunder," he cried, "this tree! Where did this tree come from? Did you do this?"

The questions stopped. Everyone looked at Wunder, silent, waiting.

And again, Wunder knew exactly what to say.

"No," he said. "It wasn't me. It was a miracle."

The word rippled through the crowd. *Miracle . . . miracle . . . miracle.* Here was the miracle that they had been told to come experience.

And now there were more questions.

"What do you mean *miracle*?"

"Why is it in a graveyard?"

"What does it mean?"

Wunder glanced across the cemetery to the DoorWay House. He wondered where the witch was. This was her moment. Everyone was here because of her. The awed peacefulness he had felt when he climbed out of the tree was fading in the face of his neighbors' bewilderment. He hadn't expected to do this on his own.

But he wasn't on his own.

"Everyone! Listen!" Faye stood in front of the tree, in front of the crowd. Her bangs were back, and her wind-blown cloak made her look, Wunder thought, like a black bird about to soar. "We're here to see the miracle of the Door-Way Tree. We're here to be with one another. We're here to be with the dead. Et cetera!"

Wunder nodded, Faye's presence and words making him

291

braver. "All of us here," he said, "have experienced miracles in our lives, miracles that we sometimes forget. This tree is here to remind us. And it's here to show us the miracles of memory and love. It's here to connect us to one another and to the ones we've lost."

"How?" cried the minister.

"Come and take a flower," Faye told him. "You'll feel it."

He didn't move. No one did. Wunder thought of the witch's words as he picked one of the blossoms: *It is easy to reach for one another in the brightness.* There was a miracle right in front of them, so bright and clear and real. And there were friends and neighbors and loved ones standing right next to them, each their own point of light. But Wunder knew how sadness and loneliness could block out even the brightest light.

Then Mariah Lazar stepped forward. She was holding Jayla on her hip, as big as she was, gripping her tightly with one hand. Her other hand, she held out, empty.

Wunder filled it with the flower.

"This is for Avery," he said.

"Thank you, Wunder," she said. "Thank you for everything."

Then she and her husband and her children headed toward the grave topped with the white in-flight bird. They went together to the grave of the one they had loved, the one they still loved, the one they had lost, the one who was waiting to be found. They went to be with her for a while.

And then everyone came forward.

All that morning, they came, the people of Branch Hill, more and more and more of them. Eugenia Simone. Margot Arvid. Mateo Ramos and his wife. Susan Holt and her stepdaughters. Mason Nash with his uncle. Charlotte Atkins with her brother and sisters and parents and dog. All the people that Wunder and Faye had connected to, all the people that the witch had called to the hill.

At first, the newcomers would stand and gaze up at the tree, awed by its size and its beauty. Then Wunder and Faye would tell them about the DoorWay Tree and give them a flower, and they would feel it—the miracle feeling, their own heart-bird—as they realized they weren't alone, as they realized their loved ones, alive and dead, were with them.

Some who came left and returned with urns or with heirlooms or with framed pictures. Their loved ones were not buried at the Branch Hill cemetery, but somehow they could feel them there just the same.

And some left and returned with elements of their own celebrations and rituals and rites, with marigolds, with lilies, with bowls of fruit and bowls of rice, with incense and candles, with brooms for sweeping and guitars for strumming and seeds for planting. There were many, many ways to think about death. There were many, many ways to connect with the dead.

Davy came, with Mrs. Baum. When he saw the tree, he couldn't speak for a long time.

"That's our branch?" he finally asked.

"That's our branch," Wunder said, smiling at his friend. "We did it."

Davy smiled back at him, smiled so big and wide, bigger and wider than Wunder had ever seen. Then he went to the tree himself and plucked two flowers.

"My great-grandparents are buried here," he told Wunder. "I never knew that. My mom told me this morning. These are for them." He shrugged. "And for me too, I guess."

The witch had given Faye a letter for her mother after all. Faye was sure she wouldn't come to the cemetery, but Mrs. Lee appeared while it was still early morning, and so did Grace. Faye met them with three flowers in her hands. They each took one, and then they went to Faye's grandfather's grave. Wunder watched from the top of the hill as they stood together with their arms around one another.

He was happy for Faye. He was happy for Davy. He was happy for Branch Hill. He was happy for himself.

But he was still waiting.

He was waiting for his mother. He was waiting for his father.

And they didn't come.

Another hour passed, and Faye returned to the top of the hill. There were dozens of people there now. Ladders leaned against the DoorWay Tree. Flowers fell.

"Can you believe this?" Wunder smiled at Faye. Then he caught himself. "Oh, sorry," he said. "I know you don't like my excessive smiling."

Faye shrugged. "It's not so bad," she said. "I think I've decided that the world needs people like you, Wunder. Zippy people. People who smile and mean it."

"The world needs people like *us*, Faye," Wunder told her. "The world needs people who believe in miracles."

When he hugged her, she didn't even protest. She hugged him back, there on Branch Hill, under the DoorWay Tree, where they had become friends.

Chapter 47

Wunder left after that. He couldn't wait any longer. He wondered, as he hurried home with his arms full of flowers, if anything would be changed there.

But at home, the house was cold and heavy and dark, the same as it had been. Wunder's heart sank as he saw the door to his parents' room, closed.

But his mother wasn't in there.

She was in his room.

She was sitting on the floor, a screwdriver in her hand. Her face was blotchy and shiny with tears. And the crib was in pieces all around her.

"Mom, are you okay?" Wunder asked, alarmed. He sank down next to her. "What happened?"

When she saw him, Wunder's mother pressed her hand to her mouth and let out a long shaking sob. She didn't speak. She just looked at him. She looked at him like she was seeing him for the first time in a long time, like she had missed him. Like she had desperately, desperately missed him.

She drew in a deep breath. "I thought it was time we took this down," she said, gesturing around with the screwdriver. "I'm so sorry we left it in here for so long. I'm so sorry I left you for so long. I was—I was in such a dark place. I've never been anywhere that dark." Then she started to cry. "But, Wunder, where have you been?"

Everything was so unexpected—his mother's look and her words and her presence in his room—that it took Wunder a moment to realize what she was asking. It took him a moment to realize that he had been gone for an entire night.

But even when he did, it seemed like there was more to the question. There was so much she had missed, so much she didn't know.

"The witch—" he started to say. "The tree—Milagros."

He wanted to tell her. He wanted to tell her everything.

But after not saying anything for so long, it was hard to find the words right away.

So he tried to show her.

"I have flowers," he said. "Flowers for you." He held them

297

out to her. Even in his room, away from the sun, they were stunningly white.

His mother took the flowers, and for a long time, she held them, cradled them. Then she brought them to her face and inhaled deeply. The petals brushed her cheeks. Wunder could see their light reflected in her eyes.

"These are beautiful, Wunder," she breathed. "I've never seen anything like them. Where did you get them?"

Here was another question that he knew would take a long time to answer.

"I was in the dark too," he finally replied. "But I found the brightness."

His mother started to cry again. "My miracle," she said. "My Wunder."

Then she opened her flower-filled arms, and Wunder fell into them. She ran her hands over his hair and his back, like she used to, and Wunder didn't try to stop her.

Until they heard a noise that made both of them turn.

Wunder's father was in the doorway.

"I've been out all night with the police," he said. "We were just at the cemetery. The people there—all those people—they told me Wunder was here. And I saw—I brought this." He held up a white flower. He looked very confused and very alone.

Wunder's mother didn't answer. But she pulled Wunder to her again with one arm and held out the other arm. Wunder's father stumbled over and sank to his knees.

And then Wunder felt both of his parents there, both of his parents with their arms around him. He felt how much they loved him with a great, imperfect love, a love that connected them, a love that would never end. And he didn't have to say anything at all.

The heart-bird circled slowly and softly inside him. The white flowers shone with their own light. And Wunder and his mother and his father sat on the floor with the pieces of the crib scattered around them.

They sat on the floor and they held one another and they cried.

Chapter 48

The sun had begun to set when he left the house. The roads were dry, as if the rainfall of the last night hadn't happened. The path in the woods was littered with leaves and vines, but everything was quiet, peaceful. The live oak seemed unchanged, green and alive and wrapped in the embrace of the resurrection fern.

He had been talking with his parents for hours, telling them what he was ready to tell and listening to what they were ready to say. His father had promised to come home on time from now on and had suggested they go on a road trip to visit family during Christmas vacation. Wunder's mother had brought up her transition back to work and had agreed to go to Mariah Lazar's grief group with Wunder's father.

Then they had decided that it was time to go, as a family, to the cemetery.

"But there's someone I have to see first," Wunder had said. "Alone."

His father had started to shake his head, but his mother had said, "Go ahead. We'll meet you there."

At the DoorWay House, Wunder knocked on the door. He knocked for a long time. No one answered. No bird cawed. Finally, he let himself inside.

In the long hallway, every door was open. Wunder walked past one after another and saw that they were all the same—small, empty, dust-coated rooms. Nothing more.

The parlor was unchanged, with its piano and empty bookshelves, and so was the dining room, its chandelier still swinging in that unfelt draft.

In the kitchen, the only difference was that the newspapers were gone. The table was laid bare for the first time. It was spiraled after all.

And sitting atop the spirals was *The Miraculous*.

Wunder sat on his usual rusty stool. The witch, it seemed, was gone. She had said she didn't have much time, but he hadn't really thought about that. He hadn't thought past the miracle.

At first, he felt angry. He had believed her, had trusted her at last. And she had left him.

Then he felt like crying because he didn't want her to be gone too. He had so much more to ask her, so many more questions.

He stared down at the table, tears filling his eyes, and that was when he saw it. On top of *The Miraculous* was a pen. It was an old-fashioned black fountain pen, and Wunder could picture the wrinkled hands that had held it and the sprawling script that had flowed from its tip.

He picked it up, and he opened *The Miraculous* to the first blank page, right after Entry #1306.

Entry #1307, he wrote in black, bold letters.

Wunder wrote for a long time, filling page after page. He wrote about the funeral and the Minister of Consolation. He wrote about Faye and the bird. He wrote about the DoorWay House and the letters, about the DoorWay Tree and the flowers. He wrote about Milagros.

Who had she been? An old woman? A witch? His sister? Why had she come to Branch Hill? Why had she sent those letters? And where did she go?

The more Wunder wrote, the more he realized that he might never know. But he also realized that he would never stop wondering. He would never stop asking questions. *Maybe there are other branches to climb up, other roots to follow down*, the witch had told him. There was so much more to find.

And whoever the witch had been, she had connected the dot of his soul—connected it to friends and to family and to all the love and beauty and mystery that surrounded him. She had shown him that he was not alone. She had shown him that there were miracles.

It was enough.

With great love, he signed the entry, *Wunder.*

Then he tore the pages out.

He left them on the table, with a flower on top.

At the cemetery, the gates were propped open, and inside, there were hundreds of people. Wunder watched as his neighbors climbed high up into the DoorWay Tree to pick flowers. He watched as they gave them away or held them close. He watched as they stood in clusters, arms around one another, some crying, some laughing, some kneeling. He knew what they were feeling; he knew the way their hearts were breaking and mending at the same time.

And he knew as he watched that this was only the beginning. He knew that everyone in Branch Hill would soon come to the cemetery. Everyone in Branch Hill, and maybe even beyond.

They would come to see the bright miracle of the Door-Way Tree.

And then they would stay for a while. They would stay and reach beyond their sorrow, beyond time, beyond death. They would stay and find the miracles hidden in the darkness. They would stay.

Together.

Because here was a place where the dead weren't really gone.

Here was a place where the living stood side by side.

Here was a place where roots went down deep.

Here was a place where branches reached up high.

Here was a place where miracles happened.

Here was a place where everything changed.

Behold.

Acknowledgments

Not too long ago, very few people had ever read anything I had written and very few people knew that I wanted to publish a story someday.

But now my writing world has grown and grown, and my dream has become a reality. And there are so many people to thank for that.

And so, all my gratitude to:

- My extraordinary agent, Sara Crowe, who found a home for Wunder and Faye.
- My dream of an editor, Janine O'Malley, whose vision and love for this story were everything I could have hoped for and more.

- Melissa Warten for her insightful eye and unfailing patience and enthusiasm.
- Hayley Jozwiak and Chandra Wohleber for their keen questions and attention to detail.
- Beth Clark for designing and Matt Rockefeller for illustrating the cover that perfectly captures this story's dark and bright.
- The entire team at FSG and Macmillan Children's, including Jen Besser, Katie Quinn, Alex Hernandez, Katie Halata, and many more who welcomed me with such warmth and contributed so much wisdom and talent.
- Holly McGhee and all the Pips who make me so proud to be a part of Pippin Properties.
- My many artistic, linguistic, cultural, and religious advisors, including Adrienne Kim Clark, Jin Oh, Paul and Nicole Henry, Raquel Trinidad, Liz Oleski, Brigid Misselhorn, Meagan Bell, and Irene Aunger Smith.
- Kathleen Anderson, a mentor and friend through many stages of life.
- Tonja Ewing-Gomez and all the members of A Novel Bunch for their support and encouragement.
- The Novel Nineteens, who were the writing friends I never knew I needed and now could not imagine doing this debut year without.

- The countless writers who have inspired and challenged and shaped me.
- The many teachers, librarians, and fellow authors who I have been privileged to encounter in this new and wondrous world of children's literature.
- Every single reader who picks up this story.
- My parents for their unconditional love and unwavering belief in me. And, just as importantly, for watching my kids.
- Of course, Russ for embracing the writing-during-freetime to writing-on-a-deadline shift. I carry your heart with me, and I know you carry mine.
- And finally, to Coral Mae and Everett Reef. You two are the brightest miracles in my world.

GO FISH

JESS REDMAN

What did you want to be when you grew up?
An author. Reading and writing were my passions from an early age, and I was fully devoted to them. I wanted, with all my heart, to be an author when I grew up, and I filled up notebook after notebook with stories.

When I decided to focus on writing as an adult, I started by working on Very Serious Grown-Up Fiction. But then I realized that it's the books from my childhood that are imprinted on my mind and my heart. I can picture their covers, quote first lines, remember where I was when I read them and how they made me feel and what they taught me about myself and the world. I've loved lots of books as an adult but not in the same way. Children's literature, I believe, is where I'm supposed to be.

What's your most embarrassing childhood memory?
When I was ten, I was in a school talent show. I had practiced my song for weeks, and I could sing it perfectly, but I was TERRIFIED.

On the big night, I somehow made it through most of the song. Then at the very end, I opened my mouth to belt out that top-of-my-range, showstopping final note and out came—

—this terrible gulp-burp-ribbit sort of noise!

I didn't run off the stage (although I've done that several times too). I made it behind the curtain before I burst into tears.

But you know what? No one even mentioned my gulp-burp-ribbit afterward. No one had really noticed this huge, mortifying mistake that I was beating myself up over. It was embarrassing, but it also gave me a new perspective and taught me to have more grace and kindness toward myself.

What's your favorite childhood memory?
I grew up in Philadelphia, but my maternal grandparents lived in central Florida. So every Christmas and summer, we would take a long drive down I-95. And as we drove, my mother would read aloud to us. She read *The Hobbit* and *The Westing Game* and *A Wrinkle in Time* and all *The Chronicles of Narnia*.

When I got older, I became the reader on those trips, and I took my role as storyteller very seriously. Because of this, I'm sure, I always think of stories as an experience to share, as a way to connect.

What were your hobbies as a kid? What are your hobbies now?
This is the absolute truth: The only hobbies I've ever

stuck with or been halfway decent at are reading and writing!

I've attempted to branch out many times. I tried gymnastics, soccer, piano, and saxophone as a child. I tried surfing, guitar, and knitting as an adult. And I think it's important to try new things and find creative outlets. But in the end, I always come back to reading and writing.

Did you play sports as a kid?

I played soccer one year. There were twelve of us on the Falcons. As you may know, each team has eleven players out on the field. So the Falcons always had one player on the sidelines.

Here's all you need to know about my very brief soccer career: That person was almost always me!

What was your first job, and what was your "worst" job?

Inspired by *The Babysitter's Club*, I offered my services as a babysitter when I was about thirteen years old. On my first job, the kids took out all the pots and pans and marched around the house banging on them. One little boy kept trying to flee out the back door whenever I turned my back. Those wild children would not brush their teeth. They would not go to bed. I was so happy to leave when their parents finally came back.

I did not babysit again.

I had a variety of odd jobs after that—cleaning hotel rooms, sorting mail, dispensing movie theater popcorn. And then I worked in a bookstore, which was heavenly.

What book is on your nightstand now?
I'd like to say *The One and Only Bob* by Katherine Applegate, but I don't have a copy yet. I'm working on it though!

Where do you write your books?
I don't have an office in my cozy little house, so I write at the kitchen table and, when the weather is nice, on the back porch. My children are usually at school or asleep when I write, so I don't have to worry about being interrupted.

What sparked your imagination for the term *miracologist*?
When I first started thinking about Wunder, I knew that he would be someone who believed in impossible and magical things. It slowly came to me that what I was describing were miracles—miracles of all types, from the everyday miracle of sunrise to the inexplicable miracle of a loved one healed from an illness.

I love stories that are infused with a little bit of magic, and I love characters that have quirks and unusual hobbies, so miracle-collecting was perfect. And who better to collect and study miracles than a *miracologist*? Although I, like Wunder in the first chapter of the story, did try terms like *miracler* and *miraclist* before settling on miracologist.

What challenges do you face in the writing process, and how do you overcome them?
I wrote constantly between the ages of eight and thirteen.

Nonstop, all the time. Then, for about ten years, I hardly wrote anything. I wanted to write something I loved or nothing at all.

Eventually, I realized that you have to write a lot of stuff you really, really, really don't like before you write something you love. It takes patience and persistence and trusting your own creative instincts and lots and lots of editing.

What is your favorite word?

I love the word *quintessence*. I love the way it sounds, and I love to say it—the whisper of *quin*, the sharpness of the *t*, the murmur of *essence*. *Quintessence* also happens to be the name of my next book, which comes out May 19, 2020. *Luminous* comes in at a close second.

Who is your favorite fictional character?

When I was in third grade, I used to carry a marble-cover notebook and sneak around my neighborhood, peering in windows. I wanted to be best friends with Harriet M. Welsch. I still want her to take me along on her spy route (which always seemed much more interesting than mine), and then have cake and milk and tomato sandwiches.

And I love Bilbo. I want to go on adventures and see the world with him and the dwarves and Gandalf, but then return to the Shire for a ten-course dinner and a song by the fire.

Oh, and Matilda is a favorite. We can just sit next to each other and read. Hermione can come too.

What was your favorite book when you were a kid? Do you have a favorite book now?

Just one? If I *have* to pick just one, I'd go with *A Wrinkle in Time*. It was unlike anything I'd ever read before. I loved stubborn, imperfect Meg and brilliant Charles Wallace and Mrs. Who, Mrs. Whatsit, and Mrs. Which. That book made me feel like the universe and my own mind were both bigger places than I'd realized.

I couldn't choose a favorite book now. There is so much innovative and brilliant and beautiful literature out there. It amazes me how many worlds are being created every day.

What's the best advice you have ever received about writing?

An author who I admire very much read *The Miraculous* before it was published, and she wrote me a letter. "No matter what happens with this story," she wrote, "you can be proud that you created something beautiful."

I've taken that letter out many times. The message of valuing my creative work—and myself—outside of recognition or reviews or sales has stuck with me as I continue to try to create beautiful somethings.

What advice do you wish someone had given you when you were younger?

I struggled quite a bit during adolescence. I was quirky and intense and lonely, and it felt like my emotions were always about to overwhelm me—sometimes, they did.

If I could talk to my young self, I would tell her two things: First, no one has a perfect life. Every person is going through or has gone through or will go through something difficult. Second, even though many of my struggles were common and normal, I would still tell myself to ask for help. Everyone needs help sometimes, and that's not a bad thing.

Do you ever get writer's block? What do you do to get back on track?

When I first started writing seriously, I had a job, an internship, and grad school classes. I was so busy. And that was nothing compared to how busy I became after I had kids! When I had a free moment to write, I had to sit down and get to work immediately, even if the words didn't flow well or come out sounding right.

So I've learned to write through writer's block. And thinking about my story and my characters—while I drive, while I shower, whenever I'm tempted to fiddle with my phone—keeps me inspired.

What do you want readers to remember about *The Miraculous*?

My hope is that *The Miraculous* finds its way to readers who have experienced their own losses, readers with big questions and big feelings. What I want those readers to hear is that help and hope are available from many sources and that in this world of dark and light, of grief and miracles, we are healed by connection. And I hope that *The Miraculous* helps all readers to develop greater compassion for others, and a sense of wonder and hope.

I hope readers remember Faye's words: *"Sometimes the brightest miracles are hidden in the darkest moments . . . but you have to search for them. You can't be afraid of the dark."*

What would you do if you ever stopped writing?
This is such a sad question! I will never stop writing!

But if I did, I would go back to teaching psychology and doing therapy full-time.

I'm a licensed mental health counselor, and I've worked in college counseling centers, with kids aging out of the foster care system, as a therapist at an inpatient drug and alcohol rehab, and in private practice with middle school– and high school–aged girls, which is where my heart is. As a therapist, I've had the privilege of hearing and being a part of many, many stories.

What do you consider to be your greatest accomplishment?
At a creative level, publishing this book is my greatest accomplishment. Being an author was always my dream, and now it is a reality.

At a relational level, I have two incredible children that I absolutely adore, and being their mother is the highest honor and most miraculous part of my life.

What would your readers be most surprised to learn about you?
Even though I have always wanted to be a writer, I didn't major in English or creative writing in college. During my junior year, I spent six months backpacking around the world—Australia, New Zealand, Thailand, Cambodia, India, Egypt, and many places in between until I reached Europe where I rapidly ran out of money. After that trip, I thought international relations was my calling, so I changed my major to political science.

But after a brief stint in grad school, I realized that while traveling and learning about other cultures were definitely for me, politics were not!

Discussion Questions for
THE MIRACULOUS
by Jess Redman

1. Why do you think the author chose to begin with
    the story of Wunder's first miracle? What did you
    learn about his miracle-collecting? How does the
    story prepare you for the change in Wunder in
    the next chapter? What else is introduced here
    and reappears later in the book?

2. Friendships often grow when we share our
    experiences and feelings with one another. How
    does Wunder and Faye's friendship begin? What
    connects them? Would you like to have a friend
    like Faye? Why did Wunder's friendships with
    Davy and Tomás change? Have you ever drifted
    apart from a friend?

3. Wunder and Faye have both learned traditions
    and rituals from family members and their
    communities. What kinds of traditions do the
    people in your life keep? Are they the same as
    yours or different—or the same *and* different?
    What can we learn from one another's beliefs?

4. Sometimes a change in our lives causes us to see ourselves, others, or the world in new ways. For Wunder, this change is the loss of his sister. What changes have occurred in other characters' lives? How do these changes impact them?

5. How did you feel about the Minister of Consolation when you first met him in the cemetery? How did you feel about Eugenia Simone? Why do you think they behave the way they do? Did your view of them change when you knew their stories? How can understanding more of a person's experience change our perspective of them?

6. How do you think Wunder feels when Officer Soto tells him that the old woman might be trying to sell the tree branch? How did you feel when you read that? Did it change the way you viewed the old woman?

7. After Officer Soto brings Wunder home, Wunder feels angry at his parents. Why is he angry? How have you felt toward Wunder's parents throughout the story? Do Wunder's feelings toward his parents change by the end of the story? How can you tell? Did your feelings toward them change? What might the story look

like through Wunder's mother's eyes? Or his father's?

8. How did you feel when the branch grew into a DoorWay Tree? Was it what you were expecting? What do you think happened to Wunder when he went into the hollow of the tree? What does the DoorWay Tree connect to? How does it help Wunder face and heal from the loss of his sister?

9. What is the bright miracle that the townspeople of Branch Hill see in the cemetery? What are the hidden miracles that they are able to understand as they gather together? How does seeing the miracle of the tree help them to see the hidden miracles? How does the DoorWay Tree and coming together help the townspeople with their own losses? Can you think of anything in your life that helps you see the wonderful and the impossible when things seem difficult or dark?

10. At the end of the book, we do not find out exactly who the old woman is—a witch, Wunder's sister, or something else. How did you feel about the author's decision to leave this question unanswered? How does *not* knowing fit the themes of the story? Who do you think the old woman is?

Keep reading for
a sneak peek of *Quintessence*!

CHAPTER 1

At the very center of the town of Four Points, there was a shop called the Fifth Point.

The Fifth Point was a shop, yes, but a shop that had never sold a single thing. It was small and square and brick and tucked between a coffeehouse and a launderette so that the air around it always smelled both bitter and sweet.

On each of the shop's four sides, there was a display window, with panes of glass so grimed and grubbed and smudged that nothing on display could possibly be seen. And next to each window, there was a door.

And above each door hung a wooden sign, with script that had once been glinty gold but was now tarnished and spotted. The signs all read:

The Fifth Point

And beneath:

Open by Appointment Only

How to make an appointment, the signs didn't say. What the shop sold and who owned it, the signs didn't say that either. And almost no one in Four Points knew, because almost no one in Four Points had ever been inside the Fifth Point.

But plenty of people had been above it.

Because rising out of the top of the Fifth Point was a twisting, tapering, midnight-black iron spire that blossomed—high above the other shops, high above the town of Four Points—into a star-shaped platform.

And on all four corners of the shop, welded to the roof, fixed and firm, there were ladders. Ladders with this message engraved on their eye-level rungs:

Come right up, dear souls.
See the lights above.
Grow the Light inside.

And inside the Fifth Point, someone was watching and waiting, watching and waiting, always watching and waiting for the right ones to come and see and grow.

CHAPTER 2

If the flyer had not been stuck to the school's front door, Alma Lucas would never have noticed it. She was in a hurry, after all.

Alma was in a hurry because it was the end of the school day. The bell had just rung, and the halls were filling with students, more and more with every passing second.

This was how almost every one of her episodes had happened—in these halls, full of students.

And more than anything else, Alma did not want to have another episode.

She was also distracted, even more so than usual. She was distracted because last night after dinner she'd had the Discussion with her parents. And she'd been turning the words over in her head all day long.

Over and over and over and over.

The Discussion had gone like this:

"So, Alma," her father said, lacing his fingers together the way he did when he was about to say something serious. "Let's check in. It's been three months since we moved. It's been more than two months since your last episode. How do you think you're acclimating to Four Points?"

Alma, staring at her plate of barely touched pasta, imagined herself in a vast and snow-filled tundra wearing a swimsuit. That was how she was acclimating. Like it was negative one million degrees and she was dressed for a pool party.

But she didn't want to tell her father that. She didn't want to tell him the truth. The truth, she knew, would only lead to more Discussions.

"Alma?" her father said. "Are you listening?"

"I am," Alma replied. "And I think that I'm acclimating really well. The weather's good. That's what I think."

She hadn't been smiling before, but she smiled then. It made her face feel strange, like she'd put on a very tight mask.

"I'm glad to hear that," her father said. "I'm sure you understand why your mother and I have been worried."

"I do," Alma said. "I certainly do. Who wouldn't be worried? But you shouldn't be."

Alma's father held up one finger. "We're worried about the notes from your teachers." Two fingers. "We're worried that you still don't want to leave the house." Three fingers. "We're worried that you aren't trying to make friends."

"I *am* trying," Alma replied. "I try all the time. All day. I am always, always trying to acclimate."

In the past, Alma's father had sometimes gotten a little too intense at this point in the Discussion, asking exactly *how* she was trying and exactly *what* she planned to do differently. So now Alma's mother took over.

"We know you are, Alma Llama," she said. "But three heads are better than one, am I right? So why don't we think together of new ways to try?"

Alma's mother smiled at her. Alma doubted that her mother ever felt like she was wearing a mask. Her mother was the kind of person who smiled a lot and who meant it every time.

"Maybe you could sit with a new group at lunch?" her mother suggested. "Say hello? Smile? Play a sport? Join a club? That's an easy one—why don't you join a club? Or even—even go for a walk outside?" Her chin rested on her fist, one finger tapping her lips, as if she had just come up with these ideas.

She had not just come up with these ideas. She said the same thing every time they had the Discussion.

And every time they had the Discussion, Alma reacted the way she had last night; she smiled and she nodded. She smiled and she nodded even as she felt the bright stuff inside her, the stuff that she imagined made her herself—her Alma-ness—grow dimmer and dimmer and dimmer.

Last night's Discussion ended the way it always did too. Alma's father, his forehead furrowed and his hands laced up tight again, said, "I know that the move and James going off to college have been difficult, but it is imperative that you do something, that you make an effort. This is our home now. You must try, Alma."

Alma nodded and smiled and said, "I am trying. I really am. I really, really am."

Later, she had gone up to her new room that was the wrong color and curled up under her new bedspread that was too scratchy. She had lain awake for hours, listening to the thoughts that came over and over and over, like they did every night.

She had lain awake and felt dark inside, Alma-less inside.

Because the last episode hadn't been more than two months ago, like she'd told her parents. The last episode had been the day before.

And the episodes—they were never going to stop.

And she was never going to make new friends.

And this place was never going to feel like home.

And there was nothing, nothing, nothing to be done.

So that day, the day she saw the flyer, Alma was in a hurry and she was distracted. She had leaped up from her seat and raced out of her last class as soon as the bell rang, as she always did. She was running down the hall, as she always did. Her eyes were on the finish line—the handle of the front door.

Then her hand was on the door, and her eyes were just above.

And then there were stars.